The One That Got Away

Kelly Hunter

MILLS & BOON

First published in Great Britain 2013
by Mills & Boon, an imprint of Harlequin (UK) Limited.
Harlequin (UK) Limited, Eton House, 18-24 Paradise Road,
Richmond, Surrey TW9 1SR

© Kelly Hunter 2013

ISBN: 978 0 263 23418 3

Harlequin (UK) policy is to use papers that are natural, renewable and recyclable products and made from wood grown in sustainable forests. The logging and manufacturing process conform to the legal environmental regulations of the country of origin.

Printed and bound in Great Britain
by CPI Antony Rowe, Chippenham, Wiltshire

About Kelly Hunter

Accidentally educated in the sciences, Kelly Hunter has always had a weakness for fairytales, fantasy worlds, and losing herself in a good book. Husband…yes. Children…two boys. Cooking and cleaning…sigh. Sports…no, not really—in spite of the best efforts of her family. Gardening…yes. Roses, of course. Kelly was born in Australia and has travelled extensively. Although she enjoys living and working in different parts of the world, she still calls Australia home.

Kelly's novels *Sleeping Partner* and *Revealed: A Prince and a Pregnancy* were both finalists for the Romance Writers of America RITA® Award, in the Best Contemporary Series Romance category!

Visit Kelly online at **www.kellyhunter.net**

Also by Kelly Hunter

Did you know these are also available as eBooks?
Visit www.millsandboon.co.uk

PROLOGUE

THERE were limits—but Logan couldn't remember what they were.

He lay on the bed, stripped-out and trembling, his body screaming out for oxygen and his brain not working at all. The woman splayed beneath him looked in no better condition. Boneless in the aftermath, just the occasional twitch to remind them that there was substance there, the shallow rise and fall of her chest that accompanied her breathing.

He looked to her skin; it had been flawless when he undressed her but it was flawless no more. There were marks on it now from his fingers and from the sandpapery skin of his jaw. Marks on her wrists and her waist and the silky-soft underside of *her* jaw.

He'd met her in a bar; that much he could remember. Some student hangout near the hotel he was staying at. This hotel. This was his room; he'd brought her back here. She'd given him her number but that hadn't been enough for him. The hotel nearby. He'd walked her back to it. Invited her back to his room.

And those golden eyes had seen straight through to his soul and she'd tilted her lips towards his and told him to take what he wanted, all he wanted, and more. And he'd done so and discovered himself utterly in thrall.

'Hey,' he said gruffly, and reached out to drag his thumb across her stretched and swollen lips. Their last close encounter had been the wrong side of rough, and he felt the shame of it now, the black edge of guilt encroaching on the insane pleasure that had gone before. 'You okay?'

She opened her eyes for him, and, yeah, she was okay. He smoothed her inky-black hair away from her face, tucked it behind her ear, combed it back from her temple. He couldn't stop touching her. Such a beautiful face.

He stroked her hair back, smoothed his hand over the curve of her shoulder. 'Can I get you anything?' he offered. 'Glass of water? Room service? Shower's yours if that's what you want.' Whatever she wanted, all she had to do was ask.

And she looked at him and her lips kicked up at the corners and she said, 'Whatever you just did to me... whatever that was—I want more.'

CHAPTER ONE

'YOU could marry me,' said Max Carmichael as he stared at the civic centre drawings on Evie's drawing table. The drawings were his, and very fine they were indeed. The calculations and costings were Evie's doing, and those costings were higher—far higher—than anything she'd ever worked on before.

Evie stopped chewing over the financials long enough to spare her business partner of six years a glance. Max was an architect, and a visionary one at that. Evie was the engineer—wet blanket to Max's more fanciful notions. Put them together and good things happened.

Though not always. 'Are you talking to me?'

'Yes, I'm talking to you,' said Max with what he clearly thought was the patience of a saint. 'I need access to my trust fund. To *get* access to my trust fund I either have to turn thirty or get married. I don't turn thirty for another two years.'

'I have two questions for you, Max. Why me and why now?'

'The "why you" question is easy: (a), I don't love you and you don't love me—'

Evie studied him through narrowed eyes.

'—which will make divorcing you in two years' time a lot easier. And (b), It's in MEP's best interest that you marry me.' MEP stood for Max and Evangeline Partnership, the construction company they'd formed six years ago. 'We're going to need deep pockets for this one, Evie.' Max tapped the plans spread out before them.

She'd been telling him this for the past week. The civic centre build was a gem of a project and Max's latest obsession. High-profile, progressive design brief, reputation-enhancing. But the project was situated on the waterfront, which meant pier drilling and extensive foundation work, and MEP would have to foot the bills until the first payment at the end of stage one. 'This job's too big for us, Max.'

'You're thinking too small.'

'I'm thinking within our means.' They were a small and nimble company with a permanent staff of six, a reliable pool of good subcontractors, and the business was on solid financial footing. If they landed the civic centre job they'd need to expand the business in every respect. If they got caught with a cash-flow problem, they'd be bankrupt within months. 'We need ten million dollars cash in reserve in order to take on this project, Max. I keep telling you that.'

'Marry me and we'll have it.'

Evie blinked.

'Shut your mouth, Evie,' murmured Max, and Evie brought her teeth together with a snap.

And opened them again just as quickly. 'You have a ten-million-dollar trust fund?'

'Fifty.'

'Fif— And you never thought to *mention* it?'

'Yeah, well, it seemed a long way off.'

He didn't *look* like a fifty-million-dollar man. Tall, rangy frame, brown eyes and hair, casual dresser, hard worker. Excellent architect. 'Why do you even need to *work*?'

'I *like* to work. I want this project, Evie,' he said with understated intensity. 'I don't want to wait ten years for us to build the resources to take on a project this size. This is the one.'

'Maybe,' she said cautiously. 'But we started this business as equal partners. What happens when you drop ten million dollars into kitty and I put in none?'

'We treat it as a loan. The money goes in at the beginning of the job, buffers us against the unexpected and comes out again at the end. And we'd need a pre-nup.'

'Oh, the romance of it all,' she murmured dryly.

'So you'll think about it?'

'The money or the marriage?'

'I've found that it helps a great deal to think about them together,' said Max. 'What are you doing Friday?'

'I am not marrying you on Friday,' said Evie.

'Of course not,' said Max. 'We have to wait for the paperwork. I was thinking I could take my fiancée home to Melbourne to meet my mother on Friday. We stay a couple of nights, put on a happy show, return Sunday and get married some time next week. It's a good solution, Evie. I've thought about it a lot.'

'Yeah, well, I haven't thought about it at all.'

'Take all day,' said Max. 'Take two.'

Evie just looked at him.

'Okay, three.'

It took them a week to work through all the ramifications, but eventually Evie said yes. There were provisos, of course. They only went through with the wedding if MEP's tender for the civic centre was looking good. The marriage would end when Max turned thirty. They'd have to share a house but there would be no sharing of beds. And no sex with anyone else either.

Max had balked at that last stipulation.

Discretion regarding others had been his counter offer. Two years was a long time, he'd argued. She didn't want him all tense and surly for the next two years, did she?

Evie did not, but the role of betrayed wife held little appeal.

Eventually they had settled on *extreme* discretion regarding others, with a two-hundred-thousand-dollar penalty clause for the innocent party every time an extramarital affair became public.

'If I were a cunning woman, I'd employ a handful of women to throw themselves at you to the point where you couldn't resist,' said Evie as they headed down to Circular Quay for lunch.

'If you were that cunning I wouldn't be marrying you,' said Max as they stepped from the shadow of a Sydney skyscraper into a sunny summer's day. 'What do you want for lunch? Seafood?'

'Yep. You don't look like a man who's about to inherit fifty million dollars, by the way.'

'How about now?' Max stopped, lifted his chin, narrowed his eyes and stared at the nearest skyscraper as if he were considering taking ownership of it.

'It'd help if your work boots weren't a hundred years old,' she said gravely.

'They're comfortable.'

'And your watch didn't come from the two-dollar shop.'

'It still tells the time. You know, you and my mother are going to get on just fine,' said Max. 'That's a useful quality in a wife.'

'If you say so.'

'Dear,' said Max. 'If you say so, *dear.*'

'Oh, you poor, deluded man.'

Max grinned and stopped mid pavement. He drew Evie to his side, held his phone out at arm's length and took a picture.

'Tell me about your family, again,' she said.

'Mother. Older brother. Assorted relatives. You'll be meeting them soon enough.'

She'd be meeting his mother this weekend; it was all arranged. Max showed her the photo he'd just taken. 'What do you reckon? Tell her now?'

'Yes.' They'd had this discussion before. 'Now would be good.'

Max returned his attention to the phone, texting some kind of message to go with the photo. 'Done,' he muttered. 'Now I feel woozy.'

'Probably hunger,' said Evie.

'Don't you feel woozy?'

'Not yet. For that to happen there would need to be champagne.'

So when they got to the restaurant and ordered the seafood platter for lunch, Max also ordered champagne, and they toasted the business, the civic centre project and finally themselves.

'How come it doesn't bother you?' asked Max, when the food was gone and the first bottle of champagne had been replaced by another. 'Marrying for mercenary reasons?'

'With my family history?' she said. 'It's perfectly normal.' Her father was on his fifth wife in as many decades; her mother was on her third husband. She could count the love matches on one finger.

'Haven't you ever been in love?' he asked.

'Have you?' Evie countered.

'Not yet,' said Max as he signed for the meal, and his answer fitted him well enough. Max went through girlfriends aplenty. Most of them were lovely. None of them lasted longer than a couple of months.

'I was in love once,' said Evie as she stood and came to the rapid realisation that she wasn't wholly sober any more. 'Best week of my life.'

'What was he like?'

'Tall, dark and perfect. He ruined me for all other men.'

'Bastard.'

'That too,' said Evie with a wistful sigh. 'I was very young. He was very experienced. Worst week of my life.'

'You said best.'

'It was both,' she said with solemn gravity, and then went and spoiled it with a sloppy sucker's grin. 'Let's just call it memorable. Did I mention that he ruined me for all other men?'

'Yes.' Max put his hand to her elbow to steady her and steered her towards the stairs and guided her down them, one by one, until they stood on the pavement outside. 'You're tipsy.'

'You're right.'

'How about we find a taxi and get you home? I promise to see you inside, pour you a glass of water, find your aspirin and then find my way home. Don't say I'm not a good fiancé.'

'Vitamin B,' said Evie. 'Find that too.'

Max's phone beeped and he looked at it and grinned. 'Logan wants to know if you're pregnant.'

'Who's Logan?' Even the name was enough to cut through her foggy senses and give her pause. The devil's name had been Logan too. Logan Black.

'Logan's my brother. He's got a very weird sense of humour.'

'I hate him already.'

'I'll tell him no,' said Max cheerfully.

Minutes later, Max's phone beeped again. 'He says congratulations.'

It couldn't be her. Logan looked at the image on his phone again, at the photo Max had just sent through. Max looked happy, his wide grin and the smile in his eyes telegraphing a pleasurable moment in time. But it was the face of the bride-to-be that held and kept Logan's attention. The glossy fall of raven-black hair and the almond-shaped eyes—the tilt of them and the burnt-butter colour. She reminded him of another woman…a woman he'd worked hellishly hard to forget.

It wasn't the same woman, of course. Max's fiancée was far more angular of face and her eyes weren't quite the right shade of brown. Her mouth was more sculpted, less vulnerable…but they were of a type. A little bit fey. A whole lot of beautiful.

Entirely capable of stealing a man's mind.

Logan hadn't even known that Max was *in* a serious relationship, though, with the way Max's trust was set up and Max's recent desire to get his hands on it, he should have suspected that matrimony would be his younger half-brother's next move.

Evie, Max had called her. Pretty name.

The woman he'd known had been called Angie.

Evie. Angie. Evangeline? What were the odds?

Logan studied the photo again, wishing the background weren't so bright and their faces weren't quite so shadowed. The woman he'd known as Angie had spent the best part of a week with him. In bed, on their way to bed, in the shower after getting out of bed… She'd been young. Curious. Frighteningly uninhibited. There'd been role play. Bondage play. Too much play, and he'd instigated most of it. Crazy days and sweat-slicked nights and the stripping back of his self-control until there'd been barely enough left to walk away.

At a dead run.

He'd been twenty-five at the time, he was thirty-six now and he doubted he'd fare any better with Angie now than he had all those years ago.

He squinted. Looked at the photo again. *Could* it be Angie? They were very long odds. He'd never kept in contact with her; had no idea where she was in the world or what she was doing now.

No, he decided for the second time in as many minutes. It wasn't her. It couldn't be her.

'She pregnant?' he texted his brother.

'Hell, no,' came Max's all-caps reply, and Logan grinned and sent through his all-caps congratulations. And then deleted the picture so that he wouldn't keep staring at it and wondering what Angie—his Angie— would look like now.

* * *

Evangeline Jones felt decidedly nervous as Max helped her out of the taxi and followed her up the garden path to his mother's front door. It was one thing to agree to a marriage of convenience. It was another thing altogether to play the love-smitten fiancée in front of Max's family.

'Whose idea was this?' she muttered to Max as she stared at the elegant two-storey Victorian in front of them. 'And why did I ever imagine it was a good one?'

'Relax,' said Max. 'Even if my mother *doesn't* believe we're marrying for love, she won't mention it.'

'Maybe not to *you*,' said Evie, and then the door opened, and an elegantly dressed woman opened her arms and Max stepped into them.

Max's mother was everything a wealthy Toorak widow should be. Coiffed to perfection, her grey-blonde hair was swept up in an elegant roll and her make-up made her look ten years younger than she was. Her perfume was subtle, her jewellery exquisite. Her hands were warm and dry and her kisses were airy as she greeted Evie and then retreated a step to study her like a specimen under glass.

'Welcome to the family, Evangeline,' said Caroline, and there was no censure in that controlled and cultured voice. 'Max has spoken of you often over the years, though I don't believe we've ever met.'

'Different cities,' said Evie awkwardly. 'Please, call me Evie. Max has mentioned you too.'

'All good, I hope.'

'Always,' said Evie and Max together.

Points for harmony.

In truth, in the six years she'd known him, Max had barely mentioned his mother other than to say she'd never been the maternal type and that she set exceptionally high standards for everything; be it a manicure or the behaviour of her husbands or her sons.

'No engagement ring?' queried Caroline with the lift of an elegant eyebrow.

'Ah, no,' said Evie. 'Not yet. There was so much choice I, ah…couldn't decide.'

'Indeed,' said Caroline, before turning to Max. 'I can, of course, make an appointment for you with *my* jeweller this afternoon. I'm sure he'll have something more than suitable. That way Evie will have a ring on her finger when she attends the cocktail party I'm hosting for the pair of you tonight.'

'You didn't have to fuss,' said Max as he set their overnight cases just inside the door beside a wide staircase.

'Introducing my soon-to-be daughter-in-law to family and friends is not fuss,' said Max's mother reprovingly. 'It's expected, and so is a ring. Your brother's here, by the way.'

'You summoned him home as well?'

'He came of his own accord,' she said dryly. 'No one makes your brother do anything.'

'He's my role model,' whispered Max as they followed the doyenne of the house down the hall.

'I need a cocktail dress,' Evie whispered back.

'Get it when I go ring hunting. What kind of stone do you want?'

'Diamond.'

'Colour?'

'White.'

'An excellent choice,' said Caroline from up ahead and Max grinned ruefully.

'Ears like a bat,' he said in his normal deep baritone.

'Whisper like a foghorn,' his mother cut back, and surprised Evie by following up with a deliciously warm chuckle.

The house was a beauty. Twenty-foot ceilings and a modern renovation that complemented the building's Victorian bones. The wood glowed with beeswax shine and the air carried the scent of old-English roses. 'Did you do the renovation?' asked Evie and her dutiful fiancé nodded.

'My first project after graduating.'

'Nice work,' she said as Caroline ushered them into a large sitting room that fed seamlessly through to a wide, paved garden patio. The table there was set for four. Perfumed roses filled several large vases, their colours haphazard enough to make Evie smile.

'I had a very demanding client who knew exactly what she wanted,' said Max. 'My ego took such a beating. These days I only wish all our clients could be that specific.'

'Max tells me you're a civil engineer,' said Caroline. 'Do you enjoy your work?'

'I love it,' said Evie.

'And this new project you're quoting on? You're as enthusiastic about it as Max?'

'You mean the civic centre? Yes. It's the perfect stepping stone for us.' *Us* being the business. 'The right opportunity at exactly the right time.'

'So I hear,' said Caroline, with an enigmatic glance for her son. 'I hope it's worth it. Let me just go and tell Amelia we're ready for lunch,' she said smoothly, and swanned out of the room before anyone could reply.

'She's not buying it,' said Evie. 'The whirlwind engagement.'

'Not so,' said Max. 'She's undecided. Different beast altogether.'

'You don't take after her in looks.'

'No,' said Max. 'I take after my father.'

'You mean tall, dark, handsome and rich?' Evie teased.

'He's not rich,' said a deep voice from behind them. 'Yet.'

That voice. Such a deep, raspy baritone. Max had a deep voice too, but it wasn't like this one.

'Logan,' said Max turning around, and Evie forced herself to relax. Max had a brother called Logan; Evie knew this already. It was just a name—nothing to worry about. Plenty of Logans in this world.

And then Evie turned towards the sound of that voice too and the world as she lived in it ceased to exist, because she knew this man, this Logan who was Max's brother.

And he knew her.

'Evie, this is my brother,' said Max as he headed towards the older man. 'Logan, meet Evie.'

Manners made Evie walk puppet-like to Max's side and wait while the two men embraced. Masochism made her lift her chin and hold out her hand for Logan to shake once they were finished with the brotherly affection. He looked older. Harder. The lines on his face were more deeply etched and his bleak, black gaze was as hard as agate. But it was him.

Logan ignored her outstretched hand and shoved his hands deep into his trouser pockets instead. The movement made her memory kick. Same movement. Another time and place.

'Pretty name,' he rumbled as Evie let her arm fall to her side.

He'd known her as Angie—a name she'd once gone by. A name she'd worked hard to forget, because Angie had been needy and greedy and far too malleable beneath Logan Black's all-consuming touch.

'It's short for Evangeline,' she murmured, and met his gaze and wished she hadn't, for a fine fury had set up shop beneath his barely pleasant façade. So he'd been duped by a name. Well, so had she. She'd been expecting Logan Carmichael, brother to Max Carmichael.

Not Logan Black.

Logan's gaze flicked down over her pretty little designer dress, all the way to her pink-painted toenails peeking out from strappy summer sandals. 'Welcome to the family, *Evangeline*.'

Max wasn't stupid. He could sense the discord and he slid his arm around Evie's waist and encouraged her to tuck into his side, which she did, every bit the small, sinking ship, finding harbour.

'Thank you,' she said quietly, restricting her gaze to the buttons of Logan's casual white shirt. It wasn't the first time she'd taken shelter in Max's arms and it wasn't uncomfortable. It was just...wrong.

'How long are you staying?' Max asked his brother.

'Not long.'

Logan ran a hand through his short cropped hair and the seams of his shirt-sleeve strained over bulging triceps. Evie shifted restlessly within Max's embrace, every nerve sensitised and for all the wrong reasons.

'Did you have to travel far to get here?' she asked Logan. Not a throwaway question. She needed him to be based far, far away.

'Perth. I have a company office there. Head office is based in London. Have you ever been to London, Evangeline?'

'Yes.' She'd met him in London. Lost herself in him in London. 'A long time ago.'

'And did it meet expectations?' he asked silkily.

'Yes and no. Some of the people I met there left me cold.'

Logan's eyes narrowed warningly.

'So what is it that you do, Logan? What's your history?' Rude now, and she knew it, but curiosity would have her know what he did for a living. She'd never asked. It hadn't been that kind of relationship.

'I buy things, break them down, and repackage them for profit.'

'How gratifying,' said Evie. 'I build things.'

No mistaking the silent challenge that passed between them, or Max's silent bafflement as he stared from one to the other.

'Max, do you think your mother would mind if I took my bag up to the room?' she asked. 'I wouldn't mind freshening up.'

'Your luggage is already in your suite,' said Caroline from the doorway. 'And of course you'd like to freshen up. Come, I'll show you the way.'

Five minutes ago, Evie wouldn't have wanted to be alone with Caroline Carmichael.

Right now, it seemed like the perfect escape.

Logan watched her go, he couldn't stop himself. He remembered that walk, those legs, remembered her broken entreaties as she lay on his bed, naked and waiting. He remembered how he was with her; his breathing harsh and his brain burning. No matter how many times he'd taken her it had never been enough. Whatever she wanted, whenever she wanted it, and he hadn't recognised the danger in giving her whatever she asked for until the table had given way beneath them and Angie had cut her head on the broken table leg on the way down. 'I'm okay,' she'd said, over and over again. 'Logan, it's okay.'

Eleven years later and he could still remember the warm, sticky blood running down Angie's face, running over his hands and hers as he'd tried to determine the damage done. That particular memory was engraved on his soul.

'An accident,' she'd told the doctor at the hospital as he'd stitched her up and handed her over to the nurses to clean up her face. 'I fell.'

And then one of the nurses had eased Angie's shirt collar to one side so that she could mop up more of the blood, and there'd been bruises on Angie's skin, old ones and new, and the nurse's compassionate eyes had turned icy as she'd turned to him and said, 'I'm sorry. Could you please wait outside?'

He'd lost his lunch in the gutter on the way to get the car; still reeling from the blood on his hands and the sure knowledge that accident or not, this was *his* fault, all of it.

Like father, like son.

No goddamn control.

Angie hadn't known he was Max's brother, just now.

Logan didn't think anyone could conjure up *that* level of horrified dismay on cue. Or the hostility that had followed.

'So what was that all about?' asked Max, his easy-going nature taking a back seat to thinly veiled accusation. 'You and Evie.'

'Do you really intend to marry her?'

Do you love her, was what he *meant*.

Do you bed her? Does she scream for you the way she did for me?

'Yes,' said Max, and Logan headed for the sideboard and the decanter of Scotch that always stood ready there. He poured himself a glass and didn't stint when it came to quantity. Didn't hesitate to down the lot.

'I'm guessing that wasn't a toast,' said Max, and his voice was dry but his eyes were sharply assessing. 'What is *wrong* with you?'

'Did you protect your money? Has she signed a pre-nup?'

'Yes. And, yes. We also restructured our business partnership to reflect proportional investment. Evie's no gold-digger, Logan, if that's what you're thinking.'

'You're in *business* with her too?'

'For the past six years. She's the other half of MEP. You know this already. At least, you would if you'd been paying attention.'

'I did pay attention. I knew you had a business partner.' He'd known it was a woman. 'I just…' Didn't know it was Angie. 'So this marriage…is it just a way to get your hands on your trust money?'

A simple no was all it would take. A simple no from Max, and Logan would dredge up congratulations from somewhere and be on his way. All Max had to do was say no.

But Max hesitated.

And Logan set up a litany of swear words in his brain and reached for the decanter again.

Leave it *alone*, an inner voice urged him. It's past. It's *done*. Plenty of other women in the world. Available women. Willing women.

Angie had been willing.

'Does she *know* you're marrying her to gain access to your trust money?' he asked next.

'She knows.'

'She in love with you?'

'No. I'd never have suggested it if she was. It's only for two years. And we'll be working flat out for most of it.'

'Right. So it's just a marriage of convenience. No broken hearts to worry about at all.'

'Exactly,' said Max.

Leave it alone, Logan. Keep your big mouth shut.

But he couldn't.

No way he could have Evangeline Jones for a sister-in-law and stay sane. It was as simple as that.

'And if I said I already know your soon-to-be wife? That I met her a long time ago, long before she ever knew you? That for a week or so we were lovers?' Logan's voice sounded rough; the firewater was not, so he drank some more of it before turning to face his brother. 'What then?'

Max stared at him for what seemed like an eternity. And then turned and strode from the room without another word.

Caroline Carmichael lingered once they reached the suite; a glorious eastern-facing bedroom with en suite, bay windows overlooking the garden and a sweet little alcove stuffed with a day-bed, and alongside that a bookcase full of surprisingly well-worn books.

'It's very feminine, isn't it?' murmured Caroline. 'I've never put Max in this room before. Then again, he's never brought a fiancée home either.'

'I'm sure we'll be fine.' One big bed, one day-bed. Evie couldn't have asked for a more suitable room.

Logan Black was Max's brother. Everything was just fine.

'Because I can put you in the adjoining room if you'd rather not be together before the wedding.'

'Whatever you're comfortable with, Mrs Carmichael.' Evie made no false claim to virginity. She doubted she could have pulled it off. Besides, she could only manage one lie at a time, maybe two.

'Please, call me Caroline,' said Max's mother easily. 'It's just that it occurs to me—as Max must have known it would—that your upcoming union might be a marriage in name only. A way for Max to access the money his father left him.'

'Yes, Max warned me you might think that.'

'Oh, there's affection between you, anyone can see that,' continued Caroline as she tugged at the curtains to make them absolutely even. 'But I'm not seeing love.'

Evie eyed the other woman steadily. 'What does love look like?'

'Depends on the type,' said Caroline Carmichael. 'My first great love was Logan's father and by the time we'd left the battlefield, love looked like a wasteland. But there was passion between us, passion to burn by. My second husband knew how to coax forth a steady flame, one that warmed me through and I thanked him for it every day of his life. But you and Max... Forgive me for being so blunt, but do you really intend to share this bed?'

'None of your business, Mother,' said Max from the doorway, determination in his voice and something else. Tightness. Anger. Max so rarely got angry. 'I need to speak to Evangeline alone.'

Caroline left with a concerned glance for her son and Max shut the door behind her. Evie stayed by the bookshelf, arms crossed in front of her and her chin held high.

Surely Logan would have kept his sinner's mouth shut.

Wouldn't he?

'Logan tells me he's met you before,' said Max.

Guess not. 'Yes.'

'When?'

'Ten years ago, maybe more. I haven't kept count. We met in passing. I was on a study exchange programme at the University of Greenwich. Your brother was doing something or other in London. I never did ask what.'

'He's the one, isn't he?' said Max. 'The one who ruined you for all other men.'

'I'm thinking *ruined* is too strong a word,' said Evie. 'I was definitely exaggerating and possibly maudlin when I mentioned that to you. I'm not ruined. I don't feel ruined. Do I look ruined?'

Max took his time looking her over.

'You look flustered,' he said grimly. 'You never get flustered.'

'Not true. C'mon, Max. I had a fling with a man called Logan Black more than ten years ago. Five minutes ago you introduced him to me as your brother. I'm calling that one fluster-worthy.' Heat flooded Evie's cheeks and distress fuelled her temper. 'I'm sorry, okay? I'm sorry my past has come back into play. It was a pretty tepid past.' With one notable exception. 'It doesn't have to impact the present.'

'It just did.'

Hard to argue with that.

'Do you still want him?' asked Max.

'No.' And as if saying it louder would somehow make it true, 'NO.'

'Because he sure as hell still wants you.'

'If your brother had wanted me, Max, he'd have found me. That much I do remember about him.'

But Max just shook his head and ran his hands through his hair. He didn't look much like Logan except for his dark hair and olive skin. Their features were quite different. Their mannerisms not similar at all. No way she could have known...

'I can't believe he even told you,' she muttered. 'Why would he *do* that? What could he possibly hope to gain? Does he not like you? Is that it?'

'We get on well enough,' said Max.

'Then *why*?'

'Maybe he thought you were going to say something.'

'Yeah, well, he got that wrong.'

Max cut her a level glance. 'Honesty not really your strong suit these days, is it?'

'Or yours,' she snapped back. 'You said you had a brother—I *thought* I'd be meeting Logan Carmichael. You never told me you had a half-brother named Logan *Black*,' she said as her legs threatened to fold and she sat herself down on the day-bed. *Think, Evie. Think.* But her mind had left the building the moment she'd set eyes on Logan, and it hadn't yet returned. 'Your mother's hosting a cocktail party in our honour in just over seven hours,' she said, and put her head to her hands and the heels of her hands to her eyes and pressed down hard. 'What's the plan here? What do you want to do? Because I can go find her and apologise and tell her the engagement's off, if that's what you want.'

'Evie—'

'Or we could put in an order for a time machine. I could go back in time, find your *half*-brother and spurn his advances. Failing that, I could at least wring his neck afterwards. That'd work too.'

'Evie—'

'Because after that I'm fresh out of ideas, Max. I don't know how to fix this without making even more of a mess.' Evie's throat felt tight, her eyes started stinging. 'I didn't know. I *didn't* know he was your brother. I would *never*... If I'd known. The business.... *God.*'

The horror in Logan's eyes that last time they'd been together when she'd cut her head on the too-sharp table leg. The trembling in his hands, the fear and self-loathing in his eyes. He'd taken her to the hospital and by the time they'd arrived Logan had pulled himself together, standing silent and sombre by her side until the nurses had asked him to wait outside.

'There's no problem here,' she'd told concerned nurses firmly. 'None.'

But they'd given her a business card and on it had been a number to call and she'd shoved it in her handbag rather than argue with them any more.

Logan had taken her home and she'd known something was wrong but she hadn't been able to reach him. 'Logan, it was an accident,' she'd told him as he'd walked her to her door. 'You *know* that, right?' And she'd thought he was going to reach for her then and make everything all right, only he'd shoved his hands in his pockets instead and nodded and looked away.

Last words she'd ever said to him, because the following day Logan Black was gone from her life as if he'd never existed.

'God,' she whispered.

And then Max's hands were circling her wrists and he was crouching before her and pulling her hands away from her face. 'Hey,' he said gently. 'Drama queen. Don't go to pieces on me now. We can fix this.'

'How?'

'We just have to know what everybody's intentions are, that's all. Yours. Mine. Logan's. Because I'll stand aside if I have to, Evie, but only if there's a damn good reason for doing so.'

'That I slept with your brother isn't good enough?'

'Well, it's not ideal…' Droll, this fake fiancé of hers, when he wanted to be. 'But I've got fifty million good reasons to get over it. Question is, can you and Logan? You need to talk to him, Evie.'

'We just did. You were there. It didn't go well.'

'You need to talk to him *again*. In private. Minus the element of surprise.'

'I really don't.'

'How else are you going to know if you're over him?'

'I'm over him.'

'Yeah. And he's over you. That's why he's downstairs mainlining Scotch and you're up here falling apart.'

'He's mainlining what?'

'Says the voice of disinterest. Corner him after lunch. Let him corner you.'

'He thinks we're getting *married*, Max. He's not going to come anywhere near me.'

'I think you might be underestimating the effect you have on him, Evie. Besides, he knows this is a marriage of convenience.'

'He *what*?' Evie was having trouble keeping up with who knew what. 'How?'

'I may have mentioned it. Before he mentioned knowing you. He was concerned for me. Or possibly for you. Not sure which. He asked me straight whether our marriage was to be one of convenience.'

'You *told* him? What happened to the game plan? The "I want to pretend it's real in front of my family" plan?'

Max had the grace to look discomfited. 'Couldn't do it,' he said finally.

'You are the worst. Liar. Ever.'

'Yes, well, now we know that.' Max was getting surly, a sure sign that he'd been caught wrong-footed. 'Look, I'll go and beard my mother, tell her what's going on. But you have to talk to Logan and find out what he wants. What *you* want. See if you can imagine him as your brother-in-law.'

She really couldn't.

'Just talk to the man, Evie.'

'Okay,' she said. '*Okay.* But if I need saving, you'd better come save me.'

'I will.'

'And I'm still your business partner.'

'I know.' Max eyed her steadily. 'That's not up for renegotiation, regardless of what happens with the engagement.'

'You hold that thought,' Evie said doggedly. 'No matter what Logan tells you, you hold that thought.'

CHAPTER TWO

Evie came back downstairs five minutes later, hoping to find everyone already gathered for lunch, but there was only Logan, with his back towards her as he stared out at the garden beyond. Evie paused in the doorway, not ready for this confrontation, dead scared of this particular ghost, but he turned and there was nothing for it but to take a breath, straighten her shoulders and move forward. 'Where are the others?'

'Down in the cellar, choosing a bottle of wine,' said Logan. 'They were discussing the merits of marriages of convenience along the way. They could be a while.'

'Oh.' Happy conversations all round. And where to begin with Logan? 'I knew Max had a brother called Logan,' she said awkwardly. 'I didn't know it was you.'

'Fair enough. Now you do.'

His voice. How could she have forgotten that voice?

'What do you want from me, Logan?'

'You,' he said, and Evie's breath hitched. 'Gone.'

'We leave on Sunday.'

'From my life.'

'As far as I can be.'

'It won't be far enough, Angie. Not if you marry my brother. Not if you stay in business with him.'

'I'm not Angie,' she said with quiet firmness as thick black lashes came down to shield Logan's eyes. 'I grew up after you left me. I finished my studies and went to work on site in the construction business. I learned how to stand my ground. People call me Evie now. Evangeline when they're cross.'

'And is my brother cross with you, Evangeline?' Logan's black gaze swept up and over her, searing her. Lingering just a little too long on her hairline and the fringe that hid the faintest trace of an old, old scar.

'It's hard to say. What do you want from me, Logan? You didn't have to tell Max you'd bedded me. It's been ten years. More. Why didn't you leave that memory in the past where it belongs?'

He didn't answer her, just moved towards the drinks sideboard and poured clear liquid from a jug into two highball glasses. 'It's just water,' he said. 'Want one?'

'Thank you.'

So he picked them up and came over to her, and wasn't *that* a bad idea? Because now she could smell him and it was a scent that had haunted her, and now she could see the faint stubble on his jaw and the fine lines etched into his face. Older now, and wiser. Less inclined towards a smile.

He had a heartbreaker's smile when he chose to use it.

He held the glass out towards her and she stared at it and the strong, long fingers that held it. Go find out what he wants, had been Max's directive. Find out what you want.

So she reached for the water and deliberately brushed her fingers against Logan's in search of the fire that had once poured over her at his touch.

And came away scalded.

One sip of cool water and then another as she held Logan's gaze and fought that feeling of helplessness.

'The trouble with memories like ours,' he said roughly, 'is that you think you've buried them, dealt with them, right up until they reach up and rip out your throat.'

Some memories were like that. But not all. Sometimes memories could be finessed into something slightly more palatable.

'Maybe we could try replacing the bad with something a little less intense,' she suggested tentatively. 'You could try treating me as your future sister-in-law. We could do polite, and civil. We could come to like it that way.'

'Watching you hang off my brother's arm doesn't make me feel civilised, Evangeline. It makes me want to break things.'

Ah.

'Call off the engagement.' He wasn't looking at her. And it wasn't a request. 'Turn this mess around.'

'We need Max's trust-fund money.'

'I'll cover Max for the money. I'll buy you out.'

'What?' Anger slid through her, hot and biting. She could feel her composure slipping away but there was nothing else for it. Not in the face of the hot mess that was Logan. 'No,' she said as steadily as she could. 'No one's buying me out of anything, least of all MEP. That company is *mine*, just as much as it is Max's. I've put six years into it, eighty-hour weeks' worth of blood, sweat, tears and fears into making it the success it is. Prepping it for bigger opportunities and one of those opportunities is just around the corner. Why on earth would I let you buy me out?'

He meant to use his big body to intimidate her. Closer, and closer still, until the jacket of his suit brushed the silk of her dress but he didn't touch her, just let the heat build. His lips had that hard sensual curve about them that had haunted her dreams for years. She couldn't stop staring at them.

She needed to stop staring at them.

'You can't be in my life, Evangeline. Not even on the periphery. I discovered that the hard way ten years ago. So either you leave willingly...or I make you leave.'

'Couldn't we just—'

'No.' And then he leaned forward and brushed his lower lip against the curve of hers, and she closed her eyes and tried to pretend that her response didn't belong to her. That the thrill of pleasure that screamed through her belonged to someone else and that the hint of whisky on his lips wasn't intoxicating.

'You can't marry my brother, Angie. Don't even *think* it,' he murmured against her lips, and brought his hands up to cradle her face, and they were gentle but the tongue that stroked the seam of her mouth open was not, and the kiss that followed was not. The kiss spoke of ownership and anger and a helplessness that Evie knew all too well.

Logan's fingers tangled in her hair as he tilted her head back for better access to her mouth and the kiss continued. Not tentative. What Logan wanted, he took—that was just his nature, but the way he took it... oh...the sensual way he feasted... She'd never forgotten how deeply his enjoyment of sex had run. A pleasure seeker without equal. Giving it. Taking it. Owning it.

And then he drew back, breathing hard, and wiped the shine from her lips with his thumb, and his breath hitched and Evie plain forgot to breathe at all.

But she could still move, and she needed to move before Max and his mother returned, and there was something else she needed to know as well, so she wrapped her hand around his wrist and dug her nails into the vein, and watched for that tiny flare of pain and what he would do with it. Whether he'd resist it or chase it, and the increased pressure of his thumb crushing her lips into her teeth said chase and chase hard, but the curse that fell from his lips told of a resistance that ran equally deep.

Still fighting his own nature, then. Still that mad mix of sybarite and saint.

'You have to go,' he said.

He wasn't begging. Logan Black did not beg. But it was close.

'You hate it, don't you?' she murmured. 'What I make you want. What I make you feel. You've always hated it.'

'Yes.'

'Was that why the only place you made for me was on my knees in front of you?'

'Not *only* on your knees,' he offered roughly. 'I might be on mine.'

Which didn't help.

'Break the engagement, Angie. Find a way out of my brother's business and go far, far away. *Stay* away,' he said and abruptly let her go, moving back a step or two for good measure.

'And then what?'

'And then nothing.'

'Being left with nothing doesn't suit me these days, Logan.' Evie kept her voice steady and her back straight. No way he could know how her legs trembled and her heart thudded against her ribcage in the aftermath of his touch. 'I'm not the person you once knew. I'm stronger now. I'm a fighter now and I know what I want. The answer's no.'

'So,' said Caroline Carmichael as she swept into the room, with Max behind her brandishing a bottle of champagne in one hand and a bottle of white in the other. Evie stood on one side of the room, Logan on the other, and Caroline noted the distance between them, and probably the flush on Evie's face, with measuring eyes. 'Max mentioned we have a slight problem on our hands. I trust everything's been sorted?'

Logan said nothing. Instead, he let the silence stretch so thin you could see through it to the turmoil below.

'Well, one could hope,' said Caroline dryly. 'Do sit down to lunch, everyone. I, for one, can't problem-solve on an empty stomach. And make no mistake, this problem does need solving.' She eyed her eldest son sternly. 'Or would you prefer a fractured family?'

Logan's havoc-wreaking mouth was a thin, grim line, but he pulled out his mother's chair and saw her seated.

'Max, you'll pour?' said the widow Carmichael and Evie caught a glimpse of the iron will behind the amiable mask.

Max cracked the white and filled his mother's glass and then Evie's. 'You want me to get the Scotch?' he asked his brother.

'I'm done with the Scotch,' said Logan. 'Scotch is

for shock.' So Max filled Logan's wine glass with the pale, straw-coloured chardonnay too, and then his own.

So civilised.

They filled their plates in silence. Evie had never felt less like eating. And then Caroline looked across the table at Evie and said mildly, 'I hear you and Logan have met before.'

'Yes.' As Evie fought a blush and lost. 'It was a long time ago.'

'I heard that too,' said Caroline, and lapsed into silence while Evie sliced a spear of asparagus into half a dozen little pieces.

'It seems to me,' continued Caroline, 'that if you want this farce of a marriage to Max to continue, the best course of action would be to forget you and Logan ever met.'

'Yes,' murmured Evie. 'I thought that too.' Twelve tiny chunks of asparagus on her plate now, all lined up to make the whole. Very orderly.

'Logan?' said Max, and Evie looked up. No mistaking the question in Max's eyes or the resistance in Logan's.

'Or you can call off your engagement, I buy Evie out of your business and finance you until your trust fund comes in,' Logan told Max curtly.

'And where would that leave Evie?' asked Max.

'Gone.'

Why was there always a part of her that agreed with Logan? Why?

'I'm right here,' she said tightly. 'No need to talk around me. And you can have my share of MEP when I'm dead, Logan. I thought I made that clear. MEP is mine just as much as it is Max's and I will not give it up. Not to you. Not to anyone.'

'No one's saying you have to give it up,' said Max soothingly. 'No one but Logan's saying you have to give it up.'

Evie reached for her wine glass, only to change her mind before her fingers reached the glass. Her hands were too shaky; now was not a good time for alcohol.

'I think it's a *very* good time for alcohol,' murmured Logan, as if reading her mind.

'I'm not you,' she bit back.

'They can't even be in the same room with each other,' said Max to his mother.

'So I see,' murmured Caroline. 'Logan, I do think you're being a touch unreasonable,' she offered, before turning back to Evie. 'It's his father's fault. My first husband was utterly vulnerable to his emotions once they were roused. It used to scare him witless too.'

Only a mother could have that take on this situation. 'Logan doesn't strike me as particularly vulnerable, Mrs Carmichael.'

'Please, call me Caroline. I insist.' Caroline turned to Max. 'Do you *have* to have access your trust-fund money now?'

'We need ten million dollars to kick off the civic centre build, and they want to see our financials,' said Max. 'We've already explored several other avenues of financial backing. They weren't attractive.' Max speared Logan with a level gaze. 'Make us an offer that's attractive and Evie and I won't need to get married.'

'I just made it,' said Logan.

'Then the answer's no,' said Max with a tight shrug. 'When it comes to my marital status, I'm prepared to humour you. When it comes to MEP, Evie's an integral part of it. She stays.'

Impasse.

'Why so much float money?' asked Caroline finally. 'I don't know much about the construction industry, but it seems excessive.'

'Because we don't receive first payment until we're out of the ground on this one,' said Evie. 'It's a common enough clause in building contracts. But most of the foundation work for this particular build will have to be done underwater. Makes it expensive.'

'Sounds like you're out of your league,' said Logan.

'No, just our price range,' said Evie.

'Then get your client to advance you the funding for stage one.'

'They won't.'

'Then find another client.'

'You're right.' Evie eyed Logan steadily. 'Would you like us to build *you* an innovative, high-profile civic centre?'

'I wouldn't employ you to build me a bookshelf.'

'What do you think she *did* to him all those years ago?' Max asked his mother, dividing his gaze between her and Logan warily. 'He's not usually this intractable.'

'You should have seen him as an infant,' said Caroline. 'He could be extremely recalcitrant if he didn't get his way. I like to think I nudged it out of him. Perhaps not.'

'I'm right here,' said Logan, between gritted teeth. 'No need to talk around me.'

His mother studied Logan with sympathetic eyes. Max just studied him, and then, as if judging a walnut that would not be cracked, Max turned to Evie.

'So what'd you do to him?' asked Max. 'Did you reject him?'

'No,' said Evie quietly. 'I did everything your brother asked of me.'

'Never a good move,' said Caroline gently, and Evie shrugged and returned the older woman's gaze and thought she saw a glimmer of understanding.

'I'm still not seeing the reason for the extreme hostility,' said Max. 'You haven't seen each other in years. You were together for one week and then you parted ways. How bad can it be?'

He'd never been in thrall, thought Evie gently. He'd never known obsession. Ignorance was bliss.

'Would you like to tell him or shall I?' said Evie when the silence threatened to smother her.

'By all means, let's hear your take on it,' said Logan with exquisite politeness.

'Our time together was all-consuming,' she offered, and wore Logan's burning black gaze and didn't flinch. 'I was very...malleable, and Logan liked it that way. The combination worked a little too well for us. And then one day someone held a mirror up to our actions and Logan didn't like what he could see, and so he left and spared us both.' Evie arched a slender eyebrow and Logan met it with a bitter twist of his beautifully sculpted lips. 'Am I close?'

Logan inclined his head.

And for once, neither Max nor his mother had anything to say.

CHAPTER THREE

THE problem with the truth was that people so often hated hearing it. Logan was no exception. He didn't want to admit the darker aspects of his nature. The possessiveness. The passion that coursed through him, unbridled and deep. He'd only ever lost himself in a woman once and that was with Angie. Never again.

Not once since then.

His mother knew how dark he ran on occasion. Mothers knew. Half-brothers who were eight years the younger did not always know such things, and the furtive glances Max kept giving him set Logan to seething.

'Don't judge until you've been there,' he snapped.

'No judgment here,' said Max quickly. 'None. Just trying to figure the best way forward.'

'Get rid of her.'

'He means the best way forward for *everyone*,' his mother said pointedly.

His mother was not the weakest link at this table. Neither was Max.

Logan turned once more to Evangeline. 'You really want to cross me?'

'What I *want* is for MEP to land the civic project and for you to stop being such a dog in the manger,' she said evenly. 'You don't want me, and that's fine. I get it. I got it ten years ago when you walked away. So stay away. Stay out of my business and I'll stay out of yours.'

'You're in my *home*.'

'Actually,' his mother said gently, and reached for her wine, 'this is *my* home.'

'Logan, you'll be gone in a couple of days,' said Max carefully. 'Evie and I will be back in Sydney. Out of sight, out of mind.'

'No,' said Logan curtly. 'She won't be out of mind, she'll be within reach, and if you think your sham of a marriage will keep me in check, think again.'

'You still want her,' said Max slowly.

Logan didn't want to answer that question. For over ten years he'd avoided that particular question, contenting himself with less, always less. Touching no one too deeply and making damn sure no one tapped the darkness in him.

'Yes,' he admitted through clenched teeth, and pushed back from the table, intent on leaving before he made a bad situation worse. 'It appears I do. Which is why if you have any care for her whatsoever you'll get her the hell out of my way.'

Evie gave up all pretence of eating once Logan had stalked from the room. 'I'm sorry,' she said. 'I'm sorry.'

'Stop it, Evangeline,' said Caroline Carmichael sharply. 'When you've done wrong you can apologise. But I see no reason for you to apologise for the behaviour of my son.'

'We can call off the wedding,' said Evie. 'I'm happy to call the wedding off. This isn't going to work.'

'No kidding,' murmured Max.

'There'll be other civic centres,' she said, and almost believed it. 'Better ones.'

'Evie, you *know* how often projects like this one come up,' said Max tightly. *'Don't* lose sight of the bigger picture here for you and me and MEP. I'll talk to Logan again. He'll come round, I know he will. Because that wasn't my brother, just then. That's not who he is. He's just…jet-lagged or something.'

Evie said nothing. Caroline said nothing.

And Max drank deeply of his wine.

'Are you strong enough to withstand my eldest son's desire for you?' Caroline asked her bluntly.

'No.'

'Are you still submissive?'

'No.' Evie smiled faintly. 'I was very young. I found my strength.'

'You might want to consider ramming that particular development down Logan's throat,' said Caroline.

'I thought I just did.'

This time it was Caroline's turn to offer up a faint smile. 'Harder.'

Evie stood.

'Where are you going?' asked Max.

'To abuse your brother's throat.'

She found him in one of the bedrooms, slinging clothes into a suitcase with little care as to how they landed.

'Get out,' he said when he saw her in the doorway.

'No.' Evie made herself continue forward, shutting the door behind her, and moving forward again until she was well into the room, but not so close as to be within reach. 'You're being childish, Logan. You're letting your fear of behaviours long gone colour your vision of the present. You need to learn how to deal with the person I am now. I need to learn how to deal with you.'

'*Childish?*' he said incredulously.

Was that *really* as far as he'd got with her words? 'Don't forget fearful.'

He pinned her with a fierce gaze.

'Why else would you be running away?' she pointed out as gently as she could.

And received silence in reply.

'Do you feel guilty about some of the things we did together? Is that it? Because you shouldn't. You had my consent.'

'I know that, Angie.'

'Is it because you exposed your deepest desires to me, and I just fed them to your family?'

'Those desires started—and finished—with you. They don't belong to me any more. And, yeah. You could have kept them to yourself.'

'Maybe I thought your family needed a better explanation than the one they'd been served. I didn't realise you were only interested in being truthful up to a point.'

'You should have.'

She wanted to rattle him, Evie realised. Pick away at his anger and his armour and see what was underneath. 'You can't dominate me any more, Logan. You need to realise that.'

'I don't *want* to dominate you,' he muttered. 'I never wanted that.' He shoved his hands in his trouser pockets and looked away. 'But it happened.'

'I thought I was in love with you. Week one of an intensely sexual, sensual relationship,' she argued. 'So much to feel and to learn and, yes, my focus was on pleasing you. I like to think I'd have regained my equilibrium at some stage. That the relationship dynamic would have evened out in time. But I guess we'll never know.'

'I don't want to dwell on the past, Angie. I just want you gone from my life *now*.'

'Which is in itself an exercise in enforcing your will over mine.' Evie moved forward until she was crowding his space; nothing weak about that move. 'That seem right to you?'

'You can't marry him, Angie.'

'You really think Max would still have me after the fuss you just made?'

'He's got fifty million reasons to ignore the fuss I just made,' said Logan gruffly. 'You don't. You need to end this now.'

Logan's hand went to the back of his neck. From there, it was only too easy for Evie to let her gaze run over the hard angle of his jaw, the stubble just starting to show, and from there to his lips. A woman could fixate on those lips.

'Don't,' he warned huskily.

'Don't what?' Wonder if she could coax them open? Wonder what it would take to make them say the name Evie instead of Angie? 'Don't tempt you? Don't wonder what we might have had if you'd stuck around long enough to find out? Because I do wonder what we might have had together, Logan. I can't help it. And I'm sure as hell wondering it now.'

'Nothing good.'

'You don't know that. You barely know *me*. What if I *am* a match for you now? Ever thought of that?'

'No.'

'Maybe you should,' she cautioned gently, and

touched her fingers to his lips and he went still as a statue but he let her do it. 'What if we *could* bring this passion between us under control?'

'We'd get lost,' he muttered as her fingertips strayed to his jaw. '*I'd* get lost and I can't afford to, Angie. I can't.'

'What if I know the way?'

'Do you?' he asked, and then his hands were on her waist, dragging her towards him, and his lips crushed down on hers, desperate and tortured, no half-measures with this man and there never had been. It was all or nothing, and his kisses inflamed her as desperation turned into desire hot and sweet. And then he took his tongue to her mouth and lit an inferno.

A step backwards towards the bed for him as Evie set her palms to his chest and drank deeply of his passion and his pain. A step forward for her, and then they were falling, and he was beneath her, and his eyes were closed and his ravenous mouth never left her skin.

Her dress proved a poor barrier against Logan's clever hands, the thin shoulder straps sliding down, and then he swept the bodice down to reveal the swell of small breasts and the tips of her nipples. He set his tongue to one, and then lips, and suckled hard and Evie gasped as he took her to the edge of pain, and he knew exactly where that edge began, damn him, and when to retreat and bring pleasure coursing in its wake.

Palms to his shoulders, with only the warm cotton of his shirt in the way and she wanted his clothes gone, and hers, but when she tried to undo his shirt buttons he wouldn't let her, pushing her hands away with ruthless efficiency. 'No,' he muttered.

And then he slung his arms beneath her thighs and

slid her up and over his chest and onto his mouth and licked his way past her panties and into her, and if she thought he'd been a skilled lover ten years ago it was nothing to the expertise he wielded now.

With tongue and with hands he opened her up and drew her out, until her gasps became pleas and her pleas turned into a breathless stream of nonsense as she rode him, no room for his pleasure now, it was all about Evie, and what this man had always been able to do to her in the bedroom, and that was make sensation the only thing that mattered and self-control nothing more than a wispy memory.

This wasn't submission, she thought hazily, sliding her hands down to tangle in his hair, holding him exactly where she wanted him and it didn't take long, not long at all, before Evie shot to orgasm, wave after wave of pleasure so fierce and fine that her body arched like a hunter's bow.

He let her rest, momentarily. He let her catch one breath, maybe two, and then, just when recovery seemed possible, Logan clamped his mouth over her again and came at her sideways with his tongue and slung her skywards once more.

No control over her response whatsoever as she cried out her release and prayed she hadn't been too loud, but it wasn't submission. Evie clung to the faintest of hope that surrendering to pleasure wasn't submission. It was just...

Sensitive now as she toppled forward, her forearms landing on the bed above him and her head resting on her arms. A tremor shook her, a juddering reminder of where she'd just been and what Logan had just done to get her there.

'That wasn't submission,' she said breathlessly as she tried to think of a smooth move that would get her body back down level with *his* body.

There was none.

'I was on top,' she said as she crawled back down his body the clumsy way. 'I *am* on top.'

Which sounded lame, even to her ears.

'I could have done anything with you, Evie. *Anything,* and you'd have let me.' He worked his mouth across her nipple again and had a little party there and all she could do was whimper and strain against him and hope to hell he got it into his head to party harder. 'What *is* that if not submission?' he muttered.

'Participation,' she said. 'Participation resulting from stimulation. You need to work on your definitions.'

And she needed to work on him. Cautiously, Evie inched her way further down Logan's big body until her face was level with his and her hair fell around their faces like a curtain.

He didn't look rested or anywhere close to content. Evie closed her eyes and rested her forehead gently against his, breathing in the scent of him and the scent of her still on him. He tasted of her too, as she licked at his mouth, coaxing and cajoling until he did what she wanted, which was open for her with a groan, but when she went to undo his belt, he clamped her wrist and dragged her hand back up to his chest.

'Don't,' he said against her lips and she pulled away, just a fraction.

'Why not?'

'No condoms.'

Which sounded a lot like an excuse. 'Another way, then. Same way you did me.'

'I want—'

Yes, he did want. She could feel him rigid beneath her, digging into her. 'Hard,' she murmured.

'Yes. I want hard.' As if the admission of specific needs and desires was something to be ashamed of. 'And rough.' He licked at her lips as if soothing away fresh wounds. 'Too rough for your mouth. Don't want to hurt you.'

'Hands,' she offered. 'Yours *and* mine. Rough.'

He shuddered beneath her, but he still wouldn't let her hand go any lower than his chest. 'No.' With their lips barely touching and a shield of black lashes concealing his eyes. 'You need to leave, Angie. Now. I can't do this.'

'Why not?' She could think of plenty of reasons. They were in his mother's house. She was—supposedly—still engaged to his brother. Not that it had stopped him. And then there was this fear he had of dominating her, of hurting her, and *that* was the resistance he couldn't get past. Same reason they'd parted all those years ago.

'I don't understand you.' Evie backed off a little, pulled the straps of her dress back up her shoulders. 'Condoms can be purchased. Needs can be satisfied without anyone getting hurt. And my doing as you ask and leaving your room is *not* submission. It's listening and responding and it's action born of concern. For you. For whatever's going on in that hard head of yours.' He wouldn't meet her eyes, so she put a gentle forefinger to his chin, and leaned down and gently forced eye contact. Turmoil there, and plenty of it. Black eyes blown with darkness and desire. 'You savour me with one breath and turn me away with the next. Want to tell me what that's all about?'

'I really don't. Angie, please—'

'I know,' she said. 'Just go.'

Time to smooth down her dress with fumbling fingers and hope to hell no one saw her on the way to the guestroom. She didn't understand this man who lay so unmoving on his bed, one arm behind his head, one hand hooked over his belt as he watched her through slitted eyes, his erection still straining against his trousers. Her gaze fastened on his lips next; he had such sexy, snarly lips.

'Your mother said something about your father being a man of strong passions.' Uncontrollable passions, maybe. Caroline had implied that Logan had similar issues. Mothers knew these things. 'Are you close to him?'

'My father's dead,' answered Logan flatly.

'Oh,' she said with a grimace. 'I'm sorry. I didn't know.' So many things about this man that she didn't know.

'No great loss. He died when I was ten.' Logan closed his eyes and shut her out, put his forearm over his eyes for good measure. 'My father was an abusive, controlling bastard. When my mother finally worked up the guts to leave him—and me—he blew his brains out.'

Evie stared at him in horrified silence. What did a person say to that? Where did a person even start? 'Logan—'

'Go,' he muttered gruffly. 'Please, Evangeline, just go.'

And this time Evie complied.

CHAPTER FOUR

Logan remembered to breathe again once Angie had gone and the door snicked shut behind her. He shouldn't have told her. It wasn't something he talked about. Not with his mother, not with the psychologists his mother had taken him to once she'd had him back in her care.

It was okay to be angry, several of them had told him gently. Maybe he could examine his anger; start with the little things, they'd coaxed, while his ten-year-old self had sat there and studied his ragged, chewed-off fingernails and told them he wasn't angry, not him. Not with his father for topping himself, not with his mother for leaving them. She'd come back, hadn't she? Once the old man was gone? She'd come back for her son who was volatile, and controlling and needy, just like his father, and she'd never once called him those things, just started praising all the *other* traits he possessed and sent him to shrinks to keep the crazy in check.

Why had he *told* Angie that? Why couldn't he have left it at his father was dead?

She'd run now, if she had any sense. Away from this family. Away from *him*.

Evangeline Jones didn't understand the stakes in this game, but Logan did. He knew how it went; the breaking of a woman's will. Drip by tiny drip until it was all gone and she jumped at the sound of a footfall and flinched whenever someone moved too fast. He *knew* those games, knew every move.

Second hand.

Time to take himself in hand, thought Logan grimly as he sat up and ran his palms over his face. Do something about the want first. Take the edge off; the needy, greedy edge. Stay focused on the end game, which was staying strong and staying sane.

Hurting no one.

Hurting everyone.

Evie made it back to her room without encountering anyone. She made it to the en suite and stood there staring at the carnage Logan had wrought. Lips swollen from kisses that had gone too deep, complexion still rosy from the afterglow of good sex and her eyes dark with a mixture of shock and desire.

If a man tries to warn you over and over again that he's damaged goods he probably is.

If he tells you that he has his reasons for not wanting too hard then he probably does.

If he tells you outright that he doesn't want to hurt you, it's because he knows that some day he will. Maybe not today, or tomorrow, but he will, and he's given you fair warning.

Evie turned her back on the face in the mirror and closed her eyes and tried not to remember the crazy things Logan made her feel. Time to forget the feelings and *listen* to what the man had to say and get out of his life as best she could. Tell Max she'd see him at work on Monday, make her apologies to Caroline Carmichael and *leave*.

She stripped off her dress and her underwear and tossed them over the edge of the bath. She headed for the shower and turned it on hot and hard and stood and let the water wash away the stench of cowardice that clung to her skin.

'Walk away, Evie,' she whispered, and set her palms to the wall in front of her and her face to the spray to wash away the sting of tears. 'Run.'

And then the shower door behind her opened and Logan stepped in, fully dressed, and reached for her and she went to him without hesitation, wanting to comfort and be comforted, wanting his touch more than she wanted anything in this world. Riding that slippery slope of obsession and longing as the water poured down on them both and he pressed a condom packet into her hands and pushed her back against the wall and started kissing her.

Rough was the wrong word for what he wanted. *Intense* was a better word. All-consuming, as she helped him shed his clothes and laid hands to him, learning him all over again. Condom on and then Evie on as she put shoulders to the tiles and locked her legs around Logan's waist and he was slow and forceful as he entered her, and the skin on his jaw tasted salty and a little bit rough, but his movements weren't rough, not rough at all. His movements spoke of worship and wonder and a slamming, heartbreaking need as he claimed her body and offered up his own for her pleasure.

His touch was deft and agonisingly sensual as he cupped her and tilted her just so against him. Such tenuous control once passion came to play, and Evie was no help whatsoever, because wherever Logan led she went willingly.

He wanted her mindless to everything but his touch; and he succeeded.

He wanted her convulsing against him, with her mouth on his shoulder her only tether to this earth; and he succeeded.

She wanted him with her and this time he came when she did, eyes blazing, and his body straining, matching her gasp for gasp, with his mouth on hers, but only just, and his hand on the back of her neck as if he would never let her go.

'Sorry,' he muttered when his breath had slowed enough for speech. 'Angie, I'm sorry.'

'Don't be.'

'For the mess I made of my time with you. For the mess I'm still making.'

'Don't be.'

She unlocked her legs from around him and set toes to the floor and he held the condom on and slipped out of her and turned away. No words of affection for her, no smile of reassurance, just a need he couldn't voice and old fears made new again.

She stepped on his clothes on her way out of the shower. Looked at them and looked back at him. 'Impulsive,' she said with the tiniest of smiles.

'Always.' As he cut the water and she handed him a towel. 'Around you.'

'I try to control it,' he said gruffly, a moment later. 'I *need* to control it.'

'Yes, I guess you do.' An indirect reference to his past. The history that had shaped him. This *had* been controlled for Logan. He could get way more lost in desire than that. 'Lots of baggage, Logan.'

'More than you can handle?'

'Are you asking me to have a relationship with you?' Evie wiped her face down with the towel and started in on her dripping hair.

Logan said nothing, just slung the towel around his hips and stepped from the shower, avoiding the question, avoiding her eyes so Evie figured that for a no, and wasn't surprised. He'd retreat now, he always did, and she should have felt used and confused, but she didn't. Instead she felt sad as she let her gaze wash over his naked form. Sad for him. Sad for herself. But not abused.

She didn't even know how he came to have a body like that. What sports he played, what he did to blow off steam. The list of things she didn't know about this man seemed endless. And the list of things she did know about him was short and anything but sweet.

'Do you play sports?' she asked, and when he lifted his eyebrow at the inanity of the question she shrugged and tried not to be too distracted by the thin line of hair that ran south from his belly-button and disappeared beneath that low-slung towel.

'I climb,' he said. 'Snow and water ski whenever I get the chance. Sail catamarans competitively.'

That'd do it.

'Does this have anything to do with the amount of baggage I can carry round?' he asked with the ghost of a smile.

'No,' she replied with a rueful smile. 'I just wanted to know a little more about you, that's all. Something little. Something…'

'Normal?' he offered.

It was as good a word as any. 'I don't know what to do. From the moment I first saw you again, I haven't known what to do.' Truth, and if it signified weakness on her part then so be it.

'You need to call off this wedding, Evangeline.'

'I know that, Logan.' Evie glanced towards the shower. 'Is that what the sex was all about? A demonstration of my weakness when it comes to your touch? Because if it was, it wasn't necessary. I already knew.'

'It wasn't that.' Logan turned away to pick up his soggy clothes and wrung them out. 'It was need.'

And there was the appeal of this man and the danger in him. That stinging, searing, all-consuming need—and his fear of it.

'What if we start again?' she offered quietly. 'I call off this wedding, MEP finds some other way to finance the civic centre bid and you and I, we start again. Clean slate. You might, for example, come to Sydney one weekend and ask me out on a date. We might see a movie or go for coffee in the park. You could bring me a bunch of black-eyed daisies or a paper parasol. I might feed you chocolate-cherry mud-cake with my fingers by way of thank you.'

Logan's eyes had darkened again.

'Easy as,' she said lightly. 'And your call.' She wasn't the one carrying a dead father and a battered mother around. 'What kind of cocktail party does your mother throw? Fairly formal?'

'Yes.'

'Are you planning to attend?' she asked next.

'Are you?'

Evie nodded. 'Got to try and explain my engagement to Max away somehow.'

'Just tell them my mother made a mistake. Tell them you're celebrating a business milestone rather than a personal one.'

'Yes. Something like that.' She eyed him steadily. 'We could use your help to sell it. You could aim for civilised.'

'Yes,' he said with a smile she didn't trust at all. 'I could.' And handed her back the towel and stalked from the bathroom and then from her room without another word.

'So what happened between you and Logan?' asked Max for the umpteenth time as Evie plucked a midnight-blue gown from a clothing rack and flattened it against her body.

'We talked,' she said calmly. 'Too formal?'

'No,' said Max. 'Does he still want you to go live in Antarctica?'

'Probably,' said Evie, and withdrew a sleek little black dress from the rack. 'But he knows he can't make me, so he's just going to have to learn to live with disappointment. Too severe?'

'Yes.'

Evie draped it across her arm of potential dresses anyway. Little black dresses could be deceptive. A deceptively demure black-and-caramel-coloured dress caught her eye next. Demure could be deceptive too. 'What about this one?'

'Evie, just pick one,' said Max.

'Or I could take an early flight home and forget about your mother's cocktail party altogether,' said Evie. 'As long as we're talking contingency plans, I'm liking that one a lot.'

'No,' said Max steadily. 'We ride this one out together. Kill the speculation stone dead now.'

'Maybe you can tell them I'm gay,' murmured Evie.

'They wouldn't believe me. Not if Logan's anywhere in the room.'

'Okay, then. You can be gay.' Evie eyed a plum-coloured gown with a plunging neckline and a thigh-high side split speculatively. 'What about this one?'

'Evie, just *pick* one.' And then Max looked at the dress. 'But not that one.'

Evie slid it back on the rack. 'I vote we tell your mother's friends that we're celebrating the success of our business partnership and hopefully the beginning of bigger and better things for MEP. We smile and shake our heads and say we're sorry people got the wrong idea but we're not engaged and not about to be. We keep it simple. Deny everything.'

'You really think that's going to fly?'

'Put it this way,' she said. 'You got a better idea?'

The cocktail party was every bit as awkward as Evie thought it would be. Elegant, wealthy people, all set to welcome Evie into their lives at Caroline's behest, and politely puzzled when it became clear that they didn't have to.

Civilised. It was all so very civilised, but no midnight-blue cocktail gown in the world could shield her from Logan's powerful presence as she stood by Max's side and talked business goals and achievements with strangers.

Logan didn't approach her. He stuck to his side of

the room and Evie stuck to hers. She didn't watch him out of the corner of her eye. Instead she stuck to finding him in reflections in mirrors, of which there were plenty. In the shine of tall silver vases. How could one man assault her senses the way he did, just by being in a room? One man, dressed in black tie, just like every other man in the room.

'Evie, stop fidgeting,' said Max.

'I'm not fidgeting.'

She *was* fidgeting, so with a smothered curse she stopped.

'And swearing,' murmured Max, highly amused. 'You could stop that too.'

'I'm not—damn!' Evie swore rather than add chronic lying to her list of sins too. 'How much longer do we have to stay here?'

'Until the bitter end,' said Max cheerfully. 'I'm guessing around midnight.'

She'd been sticking to mineral water until now. Maybe it was time she swapped over to something with a little more kick. Then again, the argument against alcohol was a strong one. She'd already been quite uninhibited enough today.

'You could marry someone else,' she told Max during a moment they had to themselves—just business partners sharing a quiet moment out on the patio, drinks in hand and smiles at the ready. 'A childhood friend. Someone who knows this life and how to live it. Someone who'd be happy to accommodate you for two years and then move on.'

'Absolutely not,' said Max with a shudder. 'I'm over marriage for the time being. I might try being in love with the person next time. Just a thought.'

'How are we going to get the money for the civic centre bid?'

'Overdraft for some of it,' said Max. 'I'll put my place on the market.'

'I'll put mine on,' Evie said with a sigh. 'We're still going to come up short.'

'Business loan,' said Max bleakly. 'Here, before I forget.' He fished in his pocket and pulled out something small and round and silver-coloured, those bits of it that weren't a dazzling, glittering blue. It was a sapphire ring the size of Texas. Evie didn't understand. 'My mother wants you to have this as a memento of our engagement. Something about payment for your trouble.' He held it out towards her.

'No.' Evie took a hasty step back. 'Whatever your mother's opinions are, just…no. I'm all for forgetting we were ever engaged.'

'I told her you'd say that.' Max reached for her right hand and slipped it swiftly on her middle finger. Not her ring finger, not even the proper hand. 'She seems to think I owe you a ring. That we were engaged, however briefly, and that you deserve some kind of compensation. Wear it. Flog it. I don't care. Just take it. I'm a man in search of family harmony and my mother wants you to have it.'

'I don't want it,' muttered Evie, tugging the ring off just as swiftly as it had gone on. It was too bulky anyway. Too much the reminder of bad decisions too hastily made. 'Please, Max. Just give it back to her. Tell her I don't want it.'

But Max's attention had drifted to a point just over her shoulder, his eyes narrowing fast, and Evie knew, even before she looked over her shoulder, that Logan was heading their way. 'Take it,' she said, trying to push the ring into Max's hand, only he wasn't having it, and then Logan was upon them and Max automatically moved to make room for him.

'Change of heart?' murmured Logan, looking at the ring, and shock flared deep in his eyes; right before those same eyes turned bitter and then carefully blank.

'This isn't what it looks like.' Max's words came low and fast. 'It's not an engagement ring. We're not engaged. The wedding's off and it's staying off. You know that.'

'Where'd you get the ring?' asked Logan, and didn't wait for Max's answer. 'She give it to you? Our mother? She tell you to give it to Evangeline?'

'Yes.' Max looked uneasy. Evie *was* uneasy.

'Take it,' said Evie urgently. 'I don't want it. Would someone please just take it back?'

But Logan wanted no part of it. He knew that stone, the ocean-reef-blue of it. He'd seen it before. He looked towards the small crowd of people in the adjoining room. Those who hadn't drifted out onto the patio or into the gardens and his mother was one of them. What was she doing? What the hell was she thinking giving Evie this particular ring? She had that look about her; the one that said I'm worried about you and I'm scared of what you'll do and he wished to hell she'd just *stop looking at him like that!* Look to her own flaws, for once, and not only to his.

'Logan?' said Evie, and put her hand to his forearm to draw his attention, and something twisted deep in his gut. 'Logan, what's wrong?'

'Nothing.'

'Bull,' she snapped, calling his bluff. 'You're hurt.'

'No. It's her ring. What do I care what she does with it?'

'Logan, *who* gave your mother this ring?' Evie asked tightly.

But Logan refused to answer her.

'It's the one your father gave her, isn't it?' said Evie.

'No,' said Max.

'Doesn't matter.' He wouldn't let it matter.

'Logan, this *can't* be that ring,' continued Max doggedly. 'She wouldn't do that.'

But she had.

Max wouldn't recognise it; she'd never worn it in front of him. Different lifetime. Different family. Caroline Carmichael had got it right the second time round. A gentle, supportive husband and a loving, well-balanced child.

Max thought their mother was wonderful.

And then the bitter blackness spewed forth, and, for the second time that day, Logan let it engulf him.

'She likes to remind me of him whenever she thinks I've gone too far.' He sought Evangeline's gaze. Evangeline in the midnight-blue gown that accentuated her flawless skin and slender curves. The same skin he'd put mouth to not so long ago. The same curves he wanted to caress again with an intensity that bordered on obsession. 'Have I gone too far, Evangeline?'

'No,' she said slowly as her fist clenched around the ring. 'It's not you who's gone too far.'

And before Logan had any notion of what she was about to do, Evie twirled and flung his mother's ring into the shadowy garden, into the shrubbery far, far away.

The pregnant silence that followed threatened to engulf them all.

'Good arm,' said Max finally.

'It was given to me,' she said raggedly. 'And I've done what I wanted with it. No one needs that kind of reminder in their life. *No one.*'

He couldn't cope. Logan stared at her, his every defence shattered, and something passed between them, something dark and sticky and breathtakingly savage. He didn't cope well with emotion; his mother was right. Sometimes his feelings just got too big for him to hold.

'Excuse me,' he muttered, before he did something unforgivable like drag her from the room, lock her in his arms and never let her go. 'Excuse me, I have to go.'

Evie watched him leave, her heart so full of lead she was surprised she was still standing up. 'I did the wrong thing,' she whispered to Max. 'Said the wrong thing.'

'No,' said Max and his arms came around her comfortingly, urging her to turn and focus her stricken gaze on something other than the door Logan had just exited through. 'You did exactly the right thing. He's feeling too vulnerable, that's all. He never stays when he gets that way.'

Evie didn't want to stay either. Not that she wanted to run after Logan, because she didn't. Assuming she even caught up with him, what would she say? How was she supposed to heal hurts inflicted so long ago? If they hadn't healed by now, chances were they never would.

'Max, may we leave early too?' she asked shakily. 'I've had enough. I really have.' Of the assault on her senses and on her mind. Of the impossible situations that just kept coming, and of the helplessness she felt in the face of this family's hidden pain. 'I want to go upstairs and pack, then call a taxi.'

'Where do you want to go?' Max's usually laughing brown eyes were dark with concern.

'Back to Sydney,' she said. 'Away from here. I want to go home.'

CHAPTER FIVE

WALKING away from Logan that Saturday night at the cocktail party wasn't the hardest thing Evie had ever done. Staying sane the following week was the hardest thing she'd ever done. Sane when Max looked at her sideways and kept his mouth firmly shut. Sane as she worked on project proposals and tried not to wonder what Logan was doing and what he was thinking, and whether she'd ever see him again.

How she could have handled things better.

What she might have done to make Logan stay.

'What?' she demanded in exasperation as Max walked into her office unannounced for about the tenth time that morning.

'Touchy,' he said.

'Bite me.'

'Not my buzz,' said Max, and placed a sheet of paper on top of the drawings in front of her. 'You'd be wanting my brother for that.'

He wasn't wrong. 'I'm working,' she said and picked up the sheet and held it out for Max to take back. 'Whatever it is, you deal with it.'

'Read it,' he insisted, so Evie turned it back around with a sigh.

A bank deposit notice, but not a bank she regularly dealt with. Max's personal account, by the looks of it. With deposit into it yesterday of ten million dollars.

'Trust fund?' she asked.

'Logan.'

Evie's heart skipped a beat. 'Terms?'

'Three per cent below market interest rate.'

'Handy.'

'You don't mind?' asked Max.

'Do you?'

'He stole my fake fiancée and messed with my business plan,' said Max dryly. 'I'll take his money.'

'Yay for brotherly love,' said Evie. 'As long as the loan is between you and Logan and the money comes into the business through you alone, I have no objections.'

'That's how it'll work.'

'Lucky MEP.'

'Any other questions?' asked Max.

Evie shook her head.

'You don't want to know where Logan is? What he's been doing lately?'

She *did* want to know where Logan was and what he'd been doing lately. But she sure as hell wasn't going to ask.

'PNG,' said Max, as if reading her mind. 'Sorting out the mess some mining company has made of their operation there. Sometimes Logan troubleshoots for others. For a hefty fee.'

'The devil will have his due.'

'He's a good man, Evie.'

'I know that, Max.'

'You should call him. Might improve your mood.'

'There is *nothing* wrong with my mood.'

'Carlo would beg to disagree.'

'Carlo ordered twenty-eight thousand dollars' worth of reo we don't need,' she said curtly. 'He's lucky I let him keep his *job*.'

'And Logan thinks you meek,' muttered Max beneath his breath. 'God knows why.'

Evie knew exactly why. 'Was there anything else?'

'Could be Logan will need a place to stay for a few days when he returns at the end of the week and before he heads back to London. Could be I'm thinking of offering up my apartment for him to use while he's here.'

'Why? You think he's short of cash?' asked Evie dryly.

'What I *think*,' said Max with admirable restraint, 'is that if you want to see him again, you shouldn't wait for him to call you. Call him. Arrange something. Don't assume that he knows what he's doing when it comes to relationships, especially important ones, because he doesn't.' Max plucked the bank note from her fingers and waved it in front of her face. 'This, for example, might as well have "*Evie, I want to see you again*" written all over it.'

'But it doesn't,' she countered sweetly, and Max sighed and dug his mobile out of his pocket and started in on the touch screen before handing it to her with a flourish.

'Tell him you've been mooning over him all week and want to see him again.'

'I will *not*.'

'All right. Then tell him I want my chief engineer's head back in the game and that I'm blaming *him* for the fact that it's not.'

Evie glared at Max's hastily retreating back, silently wondering just how many problems she'd solve if she brained Max with his phone. Probably not that many.

'Tell him I said thank you,' added Max.

'Tell him yourself,' she yelled after him, and then put the phone to her ear just in time to hear the man who currently inhabited most of her dreams—sleeping and waking—say his brother's name.

Which necessitated some sort of reply.

'Um…hi. It's not Max,' she said awkwardly. 'It's Evie. Evie on Max's phone. How much did you hear?'

'Everything from "thank you" onwards.'

'Oh,' she said, more than a little relieved. 'Good. Because that about covers it. Your bank transfer came in and Max's just showed it to me and we wanted to say thank you. Which I'm sure Max will do in person when he sees you next. Thank you, that is.' And if Max said anything else to his brother about Evie's recently distracted state she'd strangle him. 'And I'd like to thank you too. The money's going to help the civic centre bid's chances a lot, and Max's set on winning it and can take it from here, and I can get on with the rest of the work and let the prima donna do his thing…so thank you.'

'You often make business phone calls like this?' asked Logan.

'Never.'

'Good to know,' he murmured.

'Bite me.'

Silence after that, heavy and waiting. Evie took a deep breath. 'Max tells me you're flying into Sydney later this week, and I was thinking…'

Evie had no idea what she was thinking.

'…I was thinking that Max probably wants to invite

you into the workplace so you can look around. Which would be fine by me. If you wanted to, that is.' Evie closed her eyes, leaned back in her chair and thumped her head repeatedly against the headrest, scrabbling for confidence in the face of Logan's silence and coming up empty. 'I was thinking you might need to be picked up from the airport. I could do that. Take you wherever you wanted to go.' Excellent. Now she was officially babbling. 'How's PNG?'

'Hot, sticky and politically messy,' he said. 'Largely bereft of plain speaking.'

Evie was largely bereft of plain speaking too.

'Would you like to have dinner with me while you're here?' she asked with her eyes closed tightly shut, and figured it for as plain spoken as she was going to get. 'I know some good casual eating places. Nothing fancy. But the food's good.'

Asking a man out on a date was hard. Harder still, when the man in question said a whole lot of nothing in reply.

'This is the part where you say yes or no,' she prompted quietly.

'I don't get into Sydney until late Friday night,' he said finally. 'There'll be a hire car waiting for me.'

Of course there would.

'And I don't need the workplace tour.'

Of course he didn't. 'Let me just find Max for you, shall I?'

'Dinner on Saturday evening I could do.'

'Pardon?' Evie was halfway to the door. She probably hadn't heard him correctly.

'Dinner,' he said. 'Saturday night. Something low-fuss and easy. That I could do.'

'There's a place called Brennan's in Darlinghurst. It's a bar and grill. Very casual.'

'I'll meet you there at 6:00 p.m.,' he said. 'Evie, I've got to go. I'm meant to be in a meeting.'

Interrupting his work. Not exactly a high priority in his life. He couldn't have made it any clearer if he'd tried. But he'd said yes to seeing her again, although God knew why.

'Bye, then,' she said. And hung up before he could, and went to tell her meddling business partner that her head—far from being back in the game—was now officially screwed.

Served Max right.

Saturday came and Evie spent the bulk of it trying to forget that she'd ever asked Logan out in the first place. She went to Coogee Beach and swam in the surf and then in the rock pool with a uni friend she often caught up with on weekends. They walked the cliff walk round to Bondi and had an ice cream and then she caught the bus home. Which still gave her three hours to fill in until six and her dinner with Logan. She put on a movie and steamed through her ironing basket and did a fast tidy-up of her apartment. And then she hit the shower and saw a slightly sunburned domestic goddess, which wasn't all bad because now she could turn up at the grill looking as if she'd been enjoying her weekend, rather than just waiting for six o' clock and Logan to come around.

No woman in her right mind would pin too many hopes on Logan.

So it was well-worn jeans and a white cotton top that gathered at the hip with a multicoloured scarf that she wore to meet him. Add to that an inexpensive blue-bead necklace, half a dozen thin silver bangles, sunglasses perched on her head and Evie figured herself plenty casual as she walked into Brennan's at five to six. If Logan didn't show…if he'd changed his mind about seeing her again…well, there was food here aplenty and she wouldn't go thirsty.

But Logan was already there when Evie arrived, sitting by himself in a corner booth with a half empty beer in front of him and lines around his eyes that told of fatigue, but he smiled when he saw her and hell if she didn't melt at the sight of it. She'd never seen him in jeans and scuffed work boots before and he wore them just as easily as he wore a custom-made suit. His shirt was black, and seemed to suck in the light and women watched him from the corner of their eyes. Watched him because he was black-eyed and beautiful and sexuality clung to him like a second skin.

He stood as she approached. He took her hand and leaned closer and kissed her cheek and then withdrew. 'First date,' he murmured. 'Easy as. That's what I'm aiming for,' he added and sat back down after she sat, and placed an elegant square box, about the size of her hand, on the table between them. 'I couldn't find any black-eyed daisies or paper parasols.'

The lid came off and the sides of the box folded down to reveal a life-sized origami hummingbird sipping from a bell-shaped flower.

'It's beautiful.' Evie leaned closer for a better look, not game to touch it, so delicate was the detail. 'Exquisite. But you didn't get this from Papua New Guinea.' This was a museum-quality offering, not a last-minute little something from a handy airport gift shop.

'No.' He gave a small shrug. 'I got it today. I know I cut you short on the phone the other day, Evangeline. It was unavoidable. I know I should have called you back. I just didn't know what to say.'

'It's okay, Logan. I don't know what I want from you either.' And it was far easier to say that in person than on the phone. Evie boxed the gift back up with gentle fingers and set it on top of her handbag in the far corner of the bench seat, far away from where the food would be placed. 'Thank you for your gorgeous gift.'

Logan shrugged, shrugging it off. Don't make such a fuss over it, he might as well have said. Doesn't mean I *care*.

He'd seemed that way with his mother too, and Max to a lesser extent. Desperately trying *not* to care about them too much. If you didn't care, they couldn't hurt you. Oh, Evie knew that defence. She knew it well.

'How was business in PNG?'

'Unpredictable,' he murmured. 'In need of a strong hand.'

'So it suited you,' she countered, and he smiled that lazy wicked smile of his, the one that made her blood heat and her pulse quicken.

'Yes.'

Hard not to admire a man who worked to his strengths. 'Are you rich?' He had to be wealthy in order to slip Max ten million so quickly, but exactly *how* wealthy was a question Evie hadn't yet asked and Logan hadn't yet answered.

'You want a monetary estimate?' he asked, and she nodded, and he named a figure that made her sit back and blink. 'I inherited money early,' he said. 'My mother handed over every last cent of my father's wealth the minute I turned eighteen and I took it and put it to work. The money doubles on a regular basis and that's the way I like it.'

'Because you never want to go hungry again?' she asked.

'Because I'm addicted to power and the wielding of it.'

'Wow,' she murmured. 'A man who owns his flaws. That's really rare.'

'I wouldn't call them flaws,' he murmured with a crooked smile. 'Exactly. What about you, Evie? Are you rich?'

'Not at all, compared to you. I own my own apartment. I can sometimes afford an expensive treat but I don't make a habit of it. As far as family goes, my father's respectably well-off but not effortlessly wealthy; probably because he's on his fifth wife. My mother was wife number three. I have twelve half siblings, no full siblings, and my mother's now on husband number three. Max thinks I have no strong ties to family and no respect whatsoever for the institution of marriage. He's probably right.'

'So if a man wanted to marry you...'

'I'd take some convincing.'

'How long did it take Max to convince you?'

'Ah, but Max had good monetary *reason* for wanting to get married. And it benefited me too. And it wouldn't have been a proper marriage anyway. It was more of a business transaction. With a two-hundred-thousand-dollar windfall clause for the injured party every time one of us strayed.'

'Honour system?' asked Logan with a touch of incredulity about him.

'No. The clause only kicked in if the straying became public knowledge.'

'And Max *agreed* to this?'

'I *know*,' said Evie, making good use of her eyelashes. 'I figured Max would be up for at least a couple of million before we were through, and that's being conservative. Your brother's got a short attention span.'

'And no contract sense whatsoever.'

'I had his back though,' murmured Evie. 'If Max got too far in debt to me I was going to start matching him, indiscretion for public indiscretion.'

Logan's eyes narrowed. Evie smiled and sipped at her just-arrived soda. 'You're pulling my leg,' he said finally.

'Someone's got to. You take life entirely too seriously.'

'No, I take *contracts* seriously. There's a difference.'

'If you say so.'

'You're sunburnt,' he said and Evie nodded agreeably.

'That's because I've been to the beach.'

'Was it good?'

'Very good.'

'Maybe there should have been sunscreen involved.'

'There was. Though possibly not enough.'

'What else do you do in your down time?' he asked.

'I like to travel. Explore new places. Even a new-to-me suburb will do.'

'On your own?'

'It's better with friends. But sometimes on my own.'

'Any special friends I need to know about?' he asked.

'You mean lovers?' she said and he nodded, his eyes

narrowing. 'No. I may not be marriage-ready, but one lover at a time will do.'

'Am I currently the one?'

'I don't know.' Time for truth and if it burned then so be it. 'I guess that's what I asked you here to find out.'

'I'm only here for a week, Evie.' His voice held a quiet warning.

'Sounds familiar.' Hers held quiet challenge. 'I like you, Logan, in case you hadn't noticed. Baggage and all. It wouldn't be a hardship to spend another week with you. Might even be fun.'

'As opposed to…'

'Intense, confusing, and ultimately heartbreaking. I'd like to think that we have enough experience between us now to keep those elements out of play.'

'You don't like intense?'

'You're right. There's a lot to be said for intensity. That one can stay.'

'You calling the shots now, Evie?'

'Only some of them. Feel free to voice your requirements too.'

'I want exclusivity,' he said.

'The feeling's mutual.'

'And freedom.'

'I'll do my freely exclusive best.'

'Obedience.'

'And sometimes you'll get it.' Evie edged closer, elbows to the table, so much for manners. 'You don't want to dominate me completely, remember? Or am I wrong about that?'

'Just keep reminding me when I forget.' He had his shoulders to the padded black vinyl of the booth bench and one arm stretched out on the table towards her.

He looked gorgeous and confident and he leaned forward with a look that spoke of barely contained hunger. 'C'm'ere.'

Evie inched closer because she wanted to. Opened her lips beneath his, because she wanted that too. The taste of him, not knowing what type of kiss she'd get from him, and she wondered if he mixed his kisses up deliberately—needy and greedy one time and slow and savouring the next. Whether he ever had a plan...

Evie *never* had a plan once he laid siege to her, but that would have to change.

Just as soon as this gentle whisper of a kiss finished.

'You talk a good game, Evie,' he murmured, and eased away slowly. 'I'm tempted to give you that week.'

'This coming week is the one on offer,' she said with a gentle smile as she sat back and browsed the blackboard menu. 'Let me know what you decide. I think I'll have the salmon, spinach leaves and pear salad. You?'

'Rib eye.'

'They do a nice one here.' Small talk to settle her nerves. And then the waiter came for their order and a side of bread arrived shortly after that and Evie nibbled on it and her stomach settled further. The civic centre bid had been submitted, she told him. Max was doing the follow-up courting. Three bread-and-butter projects were out of the ground and well under way. Plans for a luxury harbour-side residence were on the drawing board. Business as usual. Enjoyable as always, that mix of creativity and calculation. There was an eco house up in the Blue Mountains that she wanted to see. Canton tower in Guangzhou, China. Hell, why not a world tour of giant Ferris wheels and fabulous hotels?

'That what you want to do this coming week?' he asked quietly. 'Because we could.'

'Maybe *you* could,' she said after a moment's startled silence. 'The rest of us get to save for years, finesse the dream and carry the sweet scent of achievement around with us when finally such a trip comes to pass. But if it's filling this coming week that you're interested in, I still have to work seven till three, Monday to Friday. Wednesday afternoon I might be able to clear. How do you feel about roller coasters and fairy floss?'

'That's your idea of a dream date?'

'You don't like roller coasters and fairy floss?'

Logan shrugged. 'It's been a while.'

For her too. Maybe it wasn't such a good combination. 'Does Max know you're having dinner with me?'

'Not unless you told him.'

'I didn't.' Which led to the next question that needed asking. 'This week you're currently considering sharing with me—do you care if people know about it?'

'Do you?'

'No. But then, I'm not the businessman wheeler and dealer with control issues.'

'I wouldn't call them issues, exactly.'

Maybe her multimillionaire wasn't so self aware after all. 'Would you want to stay at my apartment?'

'I'm staying in a serviced apartment at the Quay,' he replied. 'You could come there.'

'Yes, but it's not your home, is it? Last time we did this I was living in a student dorm and you were living out of a hotel penthouse. We spent most of our time in that penthouse naked. Beyond our sexual compatibility I had no real sense of you as a person. And you had none of me. I wonder if that was a mistake.'

'Do you really want me in your home?' he asked.

'Yes. My bed. My kitchen in the mornings. My life. For a week.'

'What if we're not compatible?'

'Then there's nothing to worry about.' Evie sat back and regarded him solemnly. 'The question you *should* be worrying about is what if we are?'

Logan ended up at her place for coffee. No word from him yet on what he would do this coming week. No more words from Evie either, regarding their relationship. Instead she invited him in and stood back and watched him as he entered her apartment. Nothing special by his standards, but more than adequate by hers. She wondered if Logan would recognise his brother's touch when it came to the design, but if he did he didn't say anything. Max had made his early reputation by converting row upon row of inner-city warehouses into spacious three-storey apartments and this was one of them. It was how they'd met. She'd asked Max for some structural changes and he'd heard her out grudgingly. About halfway into the collaboration Max's reluctance had turned to enthusiasm.

'There's three floors,' she said. 'Kitchen, living area and utilities are on the ground floor, office and spare room on the first floor and my bedroom and living quarters are up the top.'

'You have a three-storey fire pole,' he said.

'Did I mention I like rides?'

Logan just looked at her.

'I have stairs too.' Gorgeous, floating stairs she'd designed herself—one of the modifications she'd asked of Max. She'd started out with grand plans for a minimalist lifestyle, but that was half a dozen years ago now and homely clutter had moved in. Not a show-piece, this apartment, but a home. Comfortable sofas in mismatched colours. Mismatched cushions too. Lots of colour to balance the unpainted concrete walls and exposed girders. Logan was looking up at those roof-top girders now.

'What are you looking for?' she asked.

'Trapeze.'

'Huh.' She'd never considered a trapeze before, though she had considered bungee apparatus. 'You think I'd need a net?'

'That or a last will and testament. You know, I never *once* figured you for a thrill seeker.'

'Really? You don't think me sliding so willingly up and down the pleasure-pain endorphins might have clued you in?'

Logan shrugged. 'Not sure I was thinking at all when I was with you before, Evangeline.'

'And now?'

'Well, I can still remember my name,' he said. 'That's got to be a good sign. Have you given any thought to what might happen *after* our week is up?'

'Logan, I'm not sure we're even going to get through *today*. There's still three hours of it left, and forgive me for saying so but you don't seem to want to be here.' Evie was nervous. Logan looked nervous. Hardly an ideal combination.

'It's just…this is your home.'

'Yes.' She eyed Logan speculatively. 'Logan, have you ever *been* in a woman's home before? Apart from your mother's?'

'I have aunts as well,' he murmured.

'You know what I mean.' She meant had he ever been to the home of a woman he'd bedded, or intended to bed.

'No.'

'Nervous?' She turned to a high kitchen shelf and pulled down a bottle of half-empty Scotch. Good Scotch. Glasses came next and then she unscrewed the lid and poured generously.

'You really think that's the solution?'

'I'm willing to give it a whirl,' she murmured before lifting a glass and tilting it towards him and then downing it in one hasty swallow. 'That one was for courage, and here's what we're going to do. You're going to go over to the lounge, turn on the television and channel surf until you find something you want to watch. I'm going to put some nibbles on a plate and bring them over and sit down beside you and relax. There's a slim chance you might relax too.'

'Don't count on it.'

'I'm not,' she said dryly. 'What do you think the courage was for?'

Logan shot her a smile and picked up her glass and his and the Scotch bottle too before sauntering over to the lounge.

She joined him a short time later, dimming the lights on the way. Easier to ignore all the bits and pieces she'd filled her life with after that. Not so easy to ignore the effects of Logan's nearness, the subtle scent of sandalwood on his skin. The strong, sensual shape of his lips or the ripe red colour of them. He was so very kissable.

And clearly he felt completely out of place.

Two minutes she lasted. Two minutes before her hands were roaming his chest and Logan's hands were in her hair as he laid silent, lazy siege to her mouth.

Evie knew she was coming apart under Logan's touch but there was nothing she could do to prevent it. Did he *know* how closely attuned to each other they were in their lovemaking? How rare that was? Rare for her, at any rate. Maybe for Logan it was perfectly normal. Maybe he made every woman he bedded feel as if she were the only thing that mattered to him in this world.

Maybe that was just his way.

Vocal—that was new. The husky oaths that fell from his lips like endearments. The groans that sounded like prayer.

On her back now, because that was where he wanted her, with her legs drawn up on either side of him and his mouth not leaving hers. Sinuous, his movements as he rubbed up against her. Sensuality his weapon of choice.

And he used it with devastating effect.

Kissing was easy, thought Logan. Kissing was a hell of a lot easier than talking or trying to fit into a life that was not his.

His shirt came off, and Evie's would have too, but she slid out from beneath him and pushed him back against the sofa with a palm to his chest as she straddled his hips.

'My house,' she murmured. 'My rules.'

She pushed his arms back until they rested outstretched along the back of the sofa and set her lips to his triceps and he shuddered beneath her touch and closed his eyes and let her play. Pure pleasure, no pain, and he craved this just as much as he'd ever craved the other. Such a slow and easy slide into sensation. The wet lick of tongue against sensitive skin. The brush of soft hair over hardened nipples. The slow creep of moisture and heat and the tightening of his balls when finally she freed him from his clothes and loosened her own and he slid slowly into her.

Not always rough and fighting for control. Sometimes—when the mood was upon him—he could be exquisitely, unthinkingly...

Gentle.

Evie woke the next morning in her bed. She'd lured Logan there eventually and the slight shift of her head confirmed that he hadn't yet left. He lay sleeping instead, and in the quiet half-light of dawn Evie studied the man she'd tangled with so exquisitely last night. More beautiful asleep than awake—and always had been. Less guarded when he was asleep and far more innocent-looking. Slept on his tummy with his hands beneath the pillow and his head and one knee crooked towards her. As if he'd watched her slide into slumber before surrendering to it himself.

Fanciful notion, and she knew it. The man had been sated towards the end. He would have closed his eyes and been asleep within moments, just as she had. No time for analysis of the lovemaking that had taken place. The frightening, soul-stealing beauty of it.

That was what morning-afters were for.

Slowly, so as not to wake him, Evie slid silently from the bed, slipped a robe from its hanger and headed for the stairs, no need to put it on now. She'd shower downstairs where the noise would not wake him. No need to wake him for, once she did that, Logan might go.

She had a feeling he'd want to go.

'I'd kill for coffee,' he said as her toes touched the first step.

Evie turned and found herself in receipt of a sleepy gaze that swept her from head to toe. Not the full-wattage smile; he wasn't even trying and *still* he warmed her through.

'In house or out?' she asked lightly. 'Because if you're fussy, there's a place on the corner that does fancy coffee.'

'Not fussy,' he rumbled as his eyes closed once more. Not quite awake either. 'Just need something to wake me up. Evie?' he murmured.

'What?'

'Morning.'

Logan gave himself over to a few more minutes of shut-eye before rolling onto his back and setting the heels of his hands to his face in an attempt to make his eyes stay open. He shouldn't be jet-lagged; he'd only flown in from PNG. No, the tiredness came from not being able to leave Evie alone last night. Of reaching for her one last time, and then another. Of going slow and savouring every caress.

Last night he'd been given a gift. A chance to make amends for all that had gone before, and he'd done it, replaced old memories with new. Better memories that he could examine without shame. Memories he could hold on to without feeling the stain on his soul.

He looked around the room, looking for clues as to the type of person Evie was at home and finding it in the rough concrete finish of the walls and the exposed plumbing and air-con. No hiding of mechanics behind pretty painted walls for Evie. She seemed to want to strip life back to basics so she could keep an eye on it—everything exposed, even the clothes cupboard, or what there was of it, for her clothes hung on hangers over a long stretch of metal bar, not a cupboard wall in sight. The clothes were colour co-ordinated—sort of—and clearly some thought had gone into the mix and matchability of them. Lots of black and grey, and what colours there were had a vividness about them. No pretty pastels for Evie. Clearly that wasn't her style.

He was contemplating getting out of bed but hadn't quite got there yet when Evie returned with the coffee, robe on and hair gathered casually atop her head. The robe slid off one shoulder as she set the tray down on the bed and she raised her arm to slide the robe back into place with the absent-mindedness of someone who repeated that particular action often.

'Lot of space up here,' he said as she settled down carefully on the other side of the tray.

'I know,' said Evie. 'It bothers some people. They'd rather sleep in a cave with the ceiling and walls tucked in close.' She eyed him curiously. 'Does it bother you?'

'No.' But parts of her statement did. 'What people?'

'The one or two people who've been invited up here over the past half a dozen years,' she said evenly, lifting her coffee to her lips and taking a tiny sip. 'Are you asking me how many men I've had in this bed?'

'No.' None of his business.

She looked at him and her eyebrow rose just a fraction.

'Maybe,' he admitted gruffly.

'How many would you think?'

'Not going near that one, Evie.'

'Six,' she said sweetly. 'Though not all at once.'

Six was okay. Given Evangeline's charm and enjoyment when it came to the pleasures of the flesh, six lovers in as many years was downright picky.

'Anything else you'd like to know?' she offered.

'*Really* don't want to know,' he said quickly. Only a madman would ask her for details and he had no intention of doing so, and besides…he'd *wanted* her to explore her sexuality after he'd left her, hadn't he? Wanted her to be sure of her preferences and to know her own mind.

Still did.

He looked around the room again and thought of the woman-child he'd once known and the woman Evie was now. 'Tough profession, engineering,' he said mildly.

Evie nodded, letting him change the subject.

'Why'd you choose it?'

'I wanted in on a highly paid and flexible profession that had the potential to take me anywhere. No relying on anyone else for my financial well-being or my status in society.'

That need *hadn't* started with him. At least, Logan didn't think it had. 'Why the overwhelming need for independence?'

'My mother's been a trophy wife all her life. It's hard work. Soul-destroying, at times. I guess I simply grew up *not* wanting it.'

'Is that why your bedroom's so spartan? Because you're rebelling against the perfect-homemaker label?'

'I hope not,' she murmured. 'Because that'd be stupid, considering I made this home for me. No, I just really like the minimalist aesthetic. Which is not to say I'm totally against a lavish touch at times, because I guarantee you'll find one in the bathroom. Bubble bath, scented candles, fluffy towels…'

'Sensualist,' he murmured and Evie shot him a slow smile.

'Rich, coming from you,' she said. 'I've never known anyone who savours sensuality the way you do. Who cherishes touch the way you do. Anyone would think you'd been starved of it as a child.'

'My mother wasn't demonstrative,' he offered blandly. Evie had seen for herself what kind of relationship he had with his mother. His father's hand had usually been hard and punishing, but those memories he kept to himself. Better a fist than no touch at all—that was the way the crazy ran for him at times. The reason why he'd taken so instinctively to pain play during lovemaking. He hadn't needed a psychologist to tell him the why of that.

But not last night. Last night's lovemaking with Evie had been positively, effortlessly normal.

'Do you have any plans for today?' he asked, and Evie shook her head and the vivid red silk robe slid from her shoulder again.

Pretty.

He bit into the cinnamon roll Evie had brought up with the coffee and it tasted sweet and flaky and sticky on his tongue.

'I could show you round Sydney if you feel like playing tourist,' she offered.

'Can there be jet boats on the harbour involved?'

'Yes.'

'With me at the wheel?'

'No.' Evie rolled her eyes at him. 'For that you'd have to buy the boat. Bridge climb?'

'Too slow.'

'Skydiving?' she offered next. 'I'm in a club.'

'Why am I not surprised?'

'Because you're getting to know me,' she offered dulcetly. 'But in the interests of full disclosure, we could also head for the Botanic Gardens this morning and lie on the grass and listen to buskers play lazy Sunday-morning songs. That'd work for me too. I guess it all depends.'

'On what?'

'On whether you plan to stick around and slay a few more demons this week or whether after last night you already consider them vanquished, in which case my money's on you leaving some time in the next ten minutes.'

Not only did this woman know her own mind, Logan thought uncomfortably, she also had a fair and accurate reading of his. 'Do you want me to leave?'

'No.' She was breaking the other cinnamon roll into bits and he couldn't see her eyes for eyelashes, but the steadiness of that no was reassuring.

'You said you'd give me a week,' he said.

'And I will, if that's what you want.'

She still wouldn't look at him.

'I do want,' he said and leaned forward and snaked his hand through her hair and kissed her gently, and then a whole lot more thoroughly, on the lips. 'But with wanting comes fear—of my nature and of yours and of the path we took last time. You scared me, Evie. With your compliance and with what you were prepared to give. You have no idea how much I wanted to take it *all*. And then demand more.'

'You're right,' she said quietly and the gaze she pinned on him was dark and knowing. 'I didn't know the dangers of that particular road we were on. But I do now.'

'If I break you I'll never forgive myself.'

Truth.

'You won't break me, Logan. I know what I'm doing. I've got your back.' As the gentle touch of her tongue to the corner of his mouth threatened to undo him. 'And your front.' Her hand slid slowly down his stomach, searching for stiffness and finding it. 'Your measure.'

And he prayed to God that she did.

CHAPTER SIX

SUNDAY passed in a blur of tangled limbs and bed sheets and Monday morning came around way too fast. Up at six, with Logan up and ready to head back to his serviced apartment for the day. Scalding-hot coffee and marmalade on sourdough toast as Evie slipped into her work clothes and scowled at the clock. Not a morning person after a night chock-full of Logan. Not a sensible thought left in her head other than she was determined to show him what her life was like, and that her life— on the whole—involved generous quantities of work.

Evie was a good business partner to Max and she needed Logan to see that. She lived a busy life and she wanted Logan to see that too. She wouldn't be derailed by him the way she had been before.

Half six and out of the door, locking it behind her while Logan stood at her side and waited. She'd see him tonight for dinner. His choice of restaurant this time and he'd let her know exactly what that choice was some time during the day. Not to be controlling or to keep her unsure of his plans for the evening; he just didn't know yet—this wasn't his city.

A twenty-minute walk to work for Evie, with Logan

heading in the opposite direction. They parted with little fuss, no kisses to spare.

Businesslike.

Until Logan turned back and claimed her mouth with ruthless efficiency before heading off once more, this time wearing a devil's grin.

They did this for three days and three predominantly sleepless nights.

On the fourth day Max asked Evie where his brother was and whether he'd taken Evie's brain with him.

'My brain's right here in my head,' she said, and looked at the invoices that covered her desk. Ordering the materials for the various jobs they had on wasn't her pleasure, which was why she'd given the job to Carlo in the first place, but he'd made a mess of it and she'd taken the job back in the interest of straightening things out. 'What haven't I done?'

'You forgot to order the additional tie wire for the Henderson job.'

Evie groaned. 'You know what I want more than anything in this world?'

'Your brain back?' asked Max.

'A proper project manager. A really, really good one.'

'If the civic centre job comes through you can have one,' offered Max.

Evie just looked at him through her fringe. 'Who went and got the tie wire?'

'Carlo. He put it on the account. Said to tell you "Checkmate".'

'Carlo wants a proper project manager too,' said Evie. 'I'll grovel to him later.'

'That's my girl,' said Max.

'Anything else?' Evie glanced down at her desk

once more and sighed. 'Don't answer that. I'll have this sorted by the end of the day.'

'You seeing Logan again tonight?' asked Max, with not quite the right amount of disinterest.

'He's coming over, yes.' Assuming he'd left her apartment today at all. He'd discovered her home office and she'd said he could use it. He had his own computer but he was in love with her scanner and fax and her big shiny desk.

'Do you know what he's been doing with his days while he's here?'

'I think he sleeps.' How else did a man get to be so inexhaustible throughout the night?

'Did you know he blew off a face-to-face meeting with a soviet steel baron yesterday? Told him they could reschedule in two weeks' time or have a conference call, and that it was all the same to him.'

'You don't think Logan knows what he's doing when it comes to big business?' Evie leaned back in her chair and eyed Max steadily. 'Maybe he just doesn't want to work with this man.'

'Maybe he's off his game.'

'You don't like that he's spending time with me?'

'I didn't say that. I just happen to think that he's keeping his real life at bay at the moment. Which is hardly conducive to an ongoing functional relationship.'

'Your brother doesn't want an ongoing functional relationship, Max. He wants to prove to himself that he's over me. That he has no need to be scared of me. The minute he does that he'll be gone.'

Max eyed her narrowly. 'So what's in it for you?'

Evie shrugged. 'A fascinating house guest, for a while.' Max probably wouldn't want to know this next reason but it was a definite plus to Evie's way of thinking. 'Exceptionally good sex.'

Max winced. 'Is that it?'

'Isn't that enough?' countered Evie.

'Cold, Evie.'

'Maybe,' she murmured. 'But I've decided that I can't be in love with your brother, Max. Infatuated, yes. Willing to help him overcome a few demons, yes. But I can't fall in love with him. That'd be beyond stupid.'

'You know, I had this vision in my head that if I cut you free to be with Logan that your romance would progress in somewhat traditional fashion. Dating. Getting engaged. Marriage. What about marriage?'

'Marriage is overrated.'

'You're selling yourself short, Evie. And my mother's in town as of last night and she wants to have lunch with you.'

'Pardon?'

'Consider yourself forewarned. She'll be here in about…' Max glanced at his two-dollar watch. 'Now.'

'She's coming *here*?' Evie had a sudden and irresistible urge to be not here. 'I won't be here. I'm heading out on site. Now. Right now. I'm already running late.'

'Which site?'

'The Rogers site.'

'Mick's already there.'

'He needs help.'

'He's got help.'

'*My* help.' And Evie needed to be gone when Caroline Carmichael arrived. 'What does your mother want with me? I mean…if she's after her ring back, I don't have it.'

'I found the ring, Evie. I spent half a day looking for that bloody rock. I gave it back to her.'

'Oh.' Evie digested Max's words with a frown. 'What did she do with it?'

'I'm guessing she put it back where it came from. I didn't ask.'

'She hurt him.' Hurt Logan.

'Sometimes he brings it on himself.'

'You're defending her.'

'No!' said Max curtly. And with a twisted scowl, 'Yes. She's my mother, Evie. What do you want me to say?'

Good question. 'Do you know what Logan's father did to them? What he did to himself? What he did to his *son*?'

'Do you?' asked Max quietly. 'You know what Logan's told you, Evie. That's not the whole story. If you want another side of the story, best you get it from my mother. She's not a bad person. It wouldn't kill you to hear what she has to say.'

'She hurt him, Max. By having you give me that ring she used you, confused me and stuck a knife in Logan's heart. Anything she has to say should be said to Logan, not to me.'

'He doesn't listen to her, Evie. Maybe he'll listen to you. You're closer to him than anyone's ever been.'

'And yet I'm still so very, *very* far away.' Evie ran a hand through her hair. 'Max, I can't fix this. I can barely fix what went wrong with Logan and *me*. You're asking too much. Your mother is asking too much.'

'And yet here I am,' said a cultured, feminine voice and there stood Max's mother. Logan's mother too. Caroline Carmichael in her well-preserved flesh. 'Asking for an hour of your time and an open ear. I want you to listen—I *hope* you will listen to what I have to say.'

'This wasn't fair warning.' Evie eyed Max darkly. 'You're my *business* partner. We don't bring personal matters here. Not to work.'

'We've always brought personal matters here, Evie. We tangled those threads a long time ago.'

Maybe so, but she had never thought Max would ambush her like this. She glared at him some more and then at Caroline, who stood quietly by the door, wanting more from Evie than Evie had in her heart to give.

'You're here to tell me how you failed to protect your son?' she asked acidly and felt a flush of shame when Caroline Carmichael looked her dead in the eye and said yes.

'Everyone makes mistakes, Evangeline. Mistakes that shatter your world and lose you everything you love,' said Caroline with quiet dignity and Evie felt the sharp sting of tears behind her eyes. 'Please.'

'I can't help you repair your relationship with Logan.'

'I'm not expecting you to,' said Caroline. 'I just want you to help my son be the best man he can be. I want him to realise what a good man he is. I want him to be happy.'

As far as manipulation went Caroline had nailed her good—or maybe Max had. Someone had.

'One hour. Not a minute more,' said Evie, and again Logan's mother said yes.

'Why did you make Max give me that ring?' asked Evie when they were seated at a table for two on the shady terrace of a nearby restaurant. The table wobbled ever so slightly because of the convict-laid cobblestones beneath its feet, but the water was cold and the service was speedy, and, as far as Evie was concerned, speedy was good. 'You knew Logan would recognise it.'

'You have to understand,' said Caroline. 'Logan was a heartbeat away from walking out my door that weekend and never coming back. Because of you. Because of me. Because walking away is easier than staying and dealing and if there's one thing Logan knows how to do it's walk away,' said Caroline. 'Logan was about to turn his back on his family. I had nothing to lose.'

'But why the ring? Why shove those memories in his face?'

'Because I thought I could goad Logan into finally losing his temper with me. He never has, you know. He locks it all up inside. I've been thinking for years that if I could just shatter his self-control, just *once*, that he would realise that, no matter how deeply he feels betrayed, he will *never* raise his hand in anger. Never be the man his father was.' Caroline sat back and raised an elegant hand to her neck, rubbing wearily before seeming to realise what she was doing. Her hand returned to her lap and she sat up straighter, the perfect image restored.

'Do you have any idea how much courage it takes an abused woman to pick a fight, Evangeline? *That's* how much I believe in the goodness of my son's heart. That's how strongly I believe that Logan's fear of turning out like his father is misguided. He won't. He will *never* raise his hand in anger. I believe that with all that I am.'

Evie ran a hand through her hair and nodded, not trusting herself to speak.

'I'm sorry I used you, Evie. I used Max too and I've apologised to him as well. But you have to understand...

That weekend was the closest I've ever seen Logan to breaking. I thought that if I pushed him I could finally make it happen.'

Love wasn't meant to be this complicated, thought Evie raggedly. It just wasn't. 'But he didn't break.'

'Not on me, no. Instead, you threw that ring away and cracked my son's heart wide open. I'm calling that a win.'

'You're mad,' said Evie.

'Been called that before.' Caroline Carmichael's smile didn't reach her eyes. 'Mad and useless and pathetic. I used to believe it. I don't any more.'

The waiter came with glasses and water and took their lunch order. Salad for Caroline and a sandwich for Evie. Food that wouldn't take long to prepare, food that would get this luncheon finished with fast.

'If Logan's father was such a man as you describe…' Evie couldn't believe she was about to ask such an intimate question of a woman she barely knew '…why did you marry him?'

'If I said I loved him once with all my heart you'd call me a fool. But it's the only explanation I've got.'

Which was no answer at all and for some reason made Evie want to cry. Again.

'Has Logan told you anything about his father?' asked Caroline Carmichael after a long, long pause.

'Very little.' Evie shrugged and cleared her throat. 'He told me that you left him. That you left Logan too. And then his father killed himself.'

'Did he mention that he was with his father because I was in a hospital with two cracked ribs, a broken cheekbone and internal bruising?'

No. Logan hadn't mentioned that.

'Hospital,' echoed Evie.

'Yes.'

That explained...a lot.

'When I got out of hospital I went to my sister's. I stayed there a week, getting AVO's and legal advice about how to get Logan away from his father. How to *keep* him away from his father. His father was a rich man. He could have the best legal representation money could buy and I needed to cover my bases. I couldn't afford not to do everything *right*. I was *always* coming back for my son, Evangeline. Always. I just wasn't fast enough.'

Evie said nothing. There was nothing to say.

'Do you know what the ultimate bid for control ends in, Evangeline?' asked Caroline Carmichael. 'Death. And you might think that the last one standing is the victor, but not always. Sometimes the last ones standing wear the stain of that death for the rest of our lives. The helplessness and the guilt. The control issues. The fear of ever letting anyone get close.'

'But you married again.'

'I had the best shrinks money could buy and a very understanding second husband. He died too, from cancer, and it was fast and painful. Heartbreaking in its own way. But not my fault.'

There was the guilt Caroline Carmichael spoke of. The deeply held scars that coloured her life.

My mother's not a bad person, Max had said.

'Mrs Carmichael—'

'Caroline,' said the older woman. 'Please.'

'Caroline.' The name rolled off Evie's tongue easily enough. It was hard to keep hold of her anger when her overwhelming emotion was sadness. 'I appreciate you telling me about your past, and Logan's, but please… don't pin any hopes on me and Logan staying together, or on me being able to influence his relationship with you. *I'm* not pinning any hopes on me and Logan staying together. He's here for a week and we're halfway through it already, and after that he's going to go. And while I hope very much that Logan's been able to slay a few demons when it comes to him being too dominant and me being too submissive all those years ago, I'm going to let him go.'

'You don't care for him?'

'I do care for him. It'd be so *easy* to care deeply for your son, but I can't, don't you see? Logan doesn't *want* to fall in love with me. He wants a casual, easy relationship that he can walk away from, no damage done to either of us. *That's* how Logan knows he's not the dangerously obsessed and unstable man his father was. He doesn't trust his heart in that regard. Only his actions. He walks away. You *know* that's what he'll do.'

'But he isn't walking away,' offered Caroline quietly. 'Not from you.'

'He will.' Evie took a jagged breath. 'It won't be long now.'

'He'll be back.'

'Maybe. And then he'll go again. And again. And again. Mrs Carmichael, what do you want me to say?'

'I want you to say that you'll give my son a chance. That you won't be so busy protecting your own heart that you fail to see the love pouring out of his. *Don't* go into this thinking that Logan's only move will be away from you. I think he'll surprise you. Let him surprise you.'

Evie glanced away. She didn't know what to say.

'Anything else?' Because Evie *really* wanted to be done here.

'One more thing. One more piece of advice that perhaps my second husband might give to you were he alive today. He was a good man, Evie. A loving man and he loved my Logan as if he were his own. He'd have asked you to be generous with Logan when he makes mistakes.'

'I had lunch with your mother today.'

Logan stilled and Evie felt the headache that had been coming on all afternoon pick up. Most of the conversations she'd had today hadn't gone well. Evie didn't hold out a lot of hope for this one. 'She cornered me at work. Max was in on the plan as well, though I noticed he managed to weasel his way out of the actual lunch.' Bastard.

'What did she want?' Logan asked finally, his attention seemingly fixed on the far corner of her not-so-sparkling kitchen floor.

'Mostly to apologise for using me to get to you.'

'Sounds about right.' A muscle ticced in his otherwise rigid jaw. 'What else did she want?'

'To sing your praises, I think. She did a bit of that.' Evie wasn't sure she wanted to share the entire conversation with Logan, but she could reveal bits of it. 'She wanted to know my intentions towards you.'

Logan looked up, his gaze ever so slightly incredulous. 'What did you tell her?'

'I probably should have told her to mind her own business, but I didn't. I told her you were leaving at the end of the week and that I had no idea what we were doing after that. Does that sound about right?'

Logan cleared his throat and rubbed his neck with his hand. One of Caroline's traits too, when she wasn't busy aiming for full composure. 'Something like that.'

'Max asked me what was going on between us too. We're a hot topic of conversation within your family, apparently. I told him that you were an excellent house-guest and an incredibly skilled lay.'

Logan seemed to be having trouble with speech. Which was just fine by Evie, because she didn't particularly want to talk about where their relationship was going either.

Evie picked up a slice of apple pie she'd brought home with her and handed it to him along with her smuggest smile. 'You're welcome.'

CHAPTER SEVEN

LOGAN'S week at Evie's passed in a blur of easy smiles and sweat-slicked nights. Life was good but there was no denying that he had put the real life on hold in order to be here. Work was piling up back in London and his executives had taken to calling him in the middle of the night—his time—with increasingly urgent questions about the running of his business and opportunities arising. His executive assistant was ready to strangle him. On Friday she'd not so politely told him that if he didn't have his surly self back behind his desk come Monday, she wouldn't be there either. Apparently she'd had quite enough of his executive employees begging her for word on decisions that no one but Logan had the power to make. No one else sat at Logan's desk while he was away. He'd never *stayed* away for this long before, had never needed to structure his organisation so that he could.

Something to consider.

As for Evie, she was being very...understanding. She didn't push for him to stay and, apart from that time when she'd talked about lunching with his mother, she'd made no reference to where their relationship was headed at all. As if it was the most natural thing in the world for him to breeze into and out of Evie's world and make barely a ripple.

Not meek when it came to everyday living—Evie knew how to stand her ground and more. That message had come through loud and clear. He'd watched her putting the brakes on a new project Max had wanted to bid on—a bread and butter project that Max figured they could turn a quick profit on. Evie begged to differ. The client was dodgy—notoriously late with payments and not above changing specs mid build and expecting the builder to wear the cost. There were jobs worth taking, Evie had told his brother bluntly. This one wasn't worth their effort.

Max had thrown up his hands in a sulk. Evie had lifted one eyebrow, folded her arms in front of her and murmured, 'Really?'

And half an hour later Max had been back, the dodgy bread and butter bid abandoned, head down alongside Evie's as they nutted out an alteration to the civic centre plans that scattered her kitchen bench.

No wonder Max had refused to let her go.

But Max wasn't here now and Logan had to be at the airport early in the morning and, dammit, Evie could at least acknowledge that fact with more than a nod.

And then she pulled down a bottle of tequila from a shelf in the kitchen and two shot glasses and poured until tequila threatened to spill over onto the bench.

'Got any salt?' he said.

'Happens I do.' Evie had lemons too, and he felt all of sixteen as Evie told him to make a fist. He did and watched as Evie's hand circled his wrist and she brought his fist to her mouth, a tiny, knowing smile on her face as the tip of her tongue dipped into the V between his forefinger and thumb.

She had his undivided attention as she pulled away, poured salt over the wet part and set her mouth to him again, licking the salt off in one long, lazy swipe before picking up the shot glass and swallowing the contents fast.

Lemon came next and she scrunched up her eyes and shook her head as the lemon juice went down. Party.

'Hard day at the office?' he asked as she licked then at her own hand and poured salt on and offered it to him. Logan's body kicked as he took her wrist and guided it to his mouth. He took his time, his thumb stroking slowly over the pulse at her wrist, and then he rubbed his lips along the edge of her thumb and then his tongue. And then he took teeth to her skin and nipped and felt Evie's pulse kick and her eyes glow golden.

'Ordinary day at the office,' she murmured. 'But I'm hoping for an extraordinary night.'

He licked at the salt and she downed his tequila and he slammed his lips into hers and drank it straight from her mouth and chased it down with the sweet taste of her until the salt was all gone and the tequila was gone and all he could taste was Evie.

By the time she drew away to take a shaky breath, Logan was hard as concrete and a delicate flush of arousal had moved in on Evie's cheeks.

'More,' she demanded, and sucked her lower lip into her mouth and licked it clean.

'More of what?'

'Everything.'

So he poured them another tequila and this time Evie bypassed the condiments and went straight for the alcohol and then expelled her breath as if she was breathing fire. She probably was.

'Something you want to forget?'

'No. I want to remember it all.' Evie smiled and pierced his heart. 'I'm just working up the courage to let you go. Bear with me. It's going to be harder than I thought.'

Easy words, and an easy out if he wanted to take it. Keep it light, no deep, dark emotions required. Except that sorrow lurked beneath the smile in her eyes and challenge lived there too.

'I hope the week worked for you,' she said.

'It did. Did it work for you?'

Evie shrugged, and, for the moment, the challenge in her eyes won out over sorrow and goodbye. 'You know I'm a sucker for more.'

He knew what she wanted. His gaze skated over her face, lingered on a spot covered by the fall of her glossy black hair. He couldn't see the scar but he sure as hell knew it was there.

'No table tops,' she said. 'For this we use the bed.'

And still Logan hesitated.

He'd been good all week. So very restrained. Playing at normal and it had worked. He'd wanted normal. Needed to prove to them both that he could be satisfied with it. Tonight though, he craved just that little bit…more.

They still had a few hours left. They still had the night.

And there were so many ways to spend it.

He came around to her side of the counter and pushed her back against it, got up in her space, his arms either side of her. Lips to her cheek now, the scrape of his teeth against the sensitive skin of her ear lobe, just enough to make her gasp. One hand to her throat now as he took full possession of her mouth. Finding the pulse point the better to monitor it. Tilting her head back so that his mouth fitted hers exactly the way he wanted it to.

Mine. He let that thought reach the top of the stack and his hips responded with a slow and rolling grind.

'Mine,' he said and his voice came low and savage. 'Prove it.'

Oh, he was going to.

'Stroke me,' he said, and showed her exactly how he wanted it, and he was comfortable calling the shots, God help him, he was. Hard and rough and she leaned into him and set her lips to his jaw, and her teeth to the skin of his chin and nipped, at which point he slipped just that little bit out of sync with the rest of the world. The place he entered had far more jagged edges and ruins in it and the rivers ran red with pain beneath. Evie didn't need to be told to take the tip of him between fingers and thumb and squeeze hard—she already knew how much he liked riding that bright flare of pain right back into pleasure.

Knew because she liked that ride too.

'I want control tonight.' The words came from the deepest, darkest part of him. 'Over pleasure and pain and everything in between. *All* the control.'

Evie smiled as she palmed her way down blood-engorged hardness and stroked him again with a twist to her wrist that almost made him come undone. 'Then take it.'

He swore he wouldn't take too much; that this was just a game that when played well led to extreme plea-sure for both participants. He swore to do no harm and the kitchen counter wouldn't do, so he took her by the wrist and headed for the stairs.

The bottom of the stairs saw his shoulders braced against the wall and Logan's hands cradling her cheeks as he set his lips to hers again. They had to get up the stairs without him reaching for her along the way. There were a lot of stairs. Evie strained against him, hands cupping his buttocks and pulling him against her.

'Patience,' he whispered. 'Virtue.' And devoured her mouth, his tongue searching and sweeping and his teeth taunting and teasing, memorising the taste of her, testing the surrender in her.

It took them for ever to get to the bedroom.

Hours, in Evie's estimation. Or maybe it was just that time stopped so often along the way. Stopped when Logan got to sitting on the stairs with her knees either side of him, and wrapped one of her hands around the stair railing and made her put her other palm to the wall as he licked along the lacy edge of her bra, and the bra came off and he curled his tongue around a nipple before closing his lips around her and sucking hard.

Evie whimpered as passion caught a lick of pain and burned all the brighter for it.

She returned the favour when finally he let her put her mouth to him.

And then they got to the bedroom and slowly, surely, he stripped her down until the only thing that mattered was Logan's next touch and what it would bring, and she never knew what, only that it was always exactly right.

No thought of anything but the ride as he worked her, enslaved her.

No need to ever ask for more because she already had everything she'd ever wanted and his name was

Logan and when her sky turned black he was the only thing she could see.

This, she thought when she was a mindless mess of sensation and yearning and he finally sheathed himself inside her. This man and the razor-sharp edge he brought to things.

This was what she'd been waiting for.

Evie woke in the dark, twenty minutes before Logan had set the alarm on his phone to ring. He had to get to the airport by six. By the end of the day he'd be on the other side of the world. She didn't want to dwell on how empty that made her feel.

Instead, Evie stretched her arms above her head gingerly, and straightened her legs, testing for tenderness and finding echoes of it in unexpected places. Inner thigh muscles, upper arms, her mouth…overstretched and puffy, and she sucked at her lower lip, checking for splits and finding one. She turned towards the man sleeping beside her, only he wasn't asleep. Sleepy-eyed, yes, but not asleep, his gaze roved over the parts of her not covered by the sheet, and then he rolled over onto his elbow, flicked on the lamp by the bed before sliding the sheet down her body and studying the rest of her in the soft glow cast by the lamp's light.

'Roll over,' he ordered and Evie did as she was told and let him continue his examination. 'Bruise here,' he said, and ran the pad of his thumb over the curve of her hip. 'Red here.' A touch on her buttocks; the soft underside of her upper arms.

'Feels fine,' she said and slid her hands beneath the pillow and stretched again, working out the kinks, one by one.

His fingers touched the split in the middle of her lower lip and his eyes darkened. He'd used her hard and they both knew it.

'Sorry,' he rumbled gruffly.

She prodded at the split with her tongue. Decided that within half a day it'd be gone. 'Don't be.'

Logan moved his attention to her hair next, gentle fingers sliding through it, pushing it back off her face, out of her eyes. She let him find the scar he was look-ing for. Let him run his fingers over it.

'Angie—'

He hadn't called her that all week. She knew ex-actly why that name had slipped from his lips now, but it wasn't one she wanted to hear.

'Evie,' she corrected gently and drew his hand to the curve of her cheek instead. 'Angie didn't know how to pull all the scattered pieces of herself back together after a night like last night. Evie does.'

'Who taught you?' Possessiveness in his voice and in his eyes, and Evie thrilled to it, even as she rolled away from his touch and out of the crazily mussed-up bed.

'No one person. You more than anyone. Experience.' She sat on the side of the bed with her back to him and her fingers curled around the edge of the bed. She closed her eyes, tilted her head back and stretched her back out. 'You were right about me needing more ex-perience all those years ago. Hindsight's a wonderful thing.' She turned her head to look at him, expecting turmoil in his eyes and finding it. 'I like the person I am now. I value every single experience that went into the making of her. Good and bad.'

'Evie—'

Her name bled from his lips, apology shot through

with regret. 'Logan,' she replied steadily. 'If that's regret on your lips for what we did last night I'd rather not hear it. You brought a lick of pain and a lot of intense pleasure along with your lovemaking last night and you like wielding both—don't tell me you don't—and I love it when you do. No analysis required. Can't we just leave it at that?'

So he choked on whatever he'd been about to say and asked her if she wanted coffee instead.

She said yes, and watched as he stepped into sweats that rode low on his hips and disappeared down the stairs, a picture of rumpled, extremely biddable masculinity. She didn't want coffee but Logan wanted to get away from her, or do something for her, or both, and who was Evie to argue?

She waited another moment and then rose and headed for the bathroom, somewhat tender in places, walking a little stiffly, to be sure, but nothing a shower and being up and about wouldn't fix.

A quick shower this morning, anticipating that Logan too would want to clean up and be on his way. Go back to bed after he left, she could do that, but Evie knew she wouldn't.

Strip the bed, put some washing on, get out of the apartment, maybe even go for a swim and let the waves wash away her tears. Keep moving, stay busy.

He came back with coffee just as she stepped from the shower and she towelled off fast and slipped into her dressing robe. Leave him with a picture of morning domesticity. A counterpoint to the memories they'd created last night.

Tossing the towel atop the clothes basket, Evie offered up a wry smile, took the coffee from his outstretched hand and headed back towards the bed, sitting cross-legged on it but pulling a sheet up around her legs to keep her honest before taking her first sip.

He'd made the coffee *exactly* the way she liked it.

Bastard.

She watched him pack in silence, wondering whether he still needed to collect things from the serviced apartment he'd rented for the week or whether over the course of the week he'd managed to bring everything here. He'd worked here—she knew that much. Using her home office to stay in contact with his London office and his Perth office. Getting up in the early hours of the morning when his phone rang and heading downstairs while an urgent voice on the other end of the phone demanded his attention. Rich man, but definitely still a working man with responsibilities she barely understood.

But they'd done well together this past week, nonetheless. He could be proud of that. They both could.

No need to do anything but smile once he was fully packed and his attention returned to her once more. He knelt down beside her bed and took her coffee from unprotesting hands and set it aside. He pressed butterfly kisses to the wing of her eyebrow, the curve of her cheek and finally her lips. Tender, this goodbye, and she reached up to trace his lips with her fingers, still obsessed with the shape and sensuality of them.

'Got everything?' she asked quietly.

'Yes. The rest is downstairs in your office.'

She leaned forward and kissed him lightly and then once more to savour him. 'Safe journey, Mr Black. Be happy.' Then she pulled him into a fierce hug and closed her eyes and memorised the feel of being in his arms. 'I'm happy. You need to know that I wouldn't have missed one moment of this past week. With you.'

His arms tightened around her, but he didn't speak, just buried his face in the curve of her neck, breathing in deep before slowly letting go.

And then he picked up his bag and Evie closed her eyes so that she didn't have to see the set of his shoulders or the shape of his resolve as he headed for the stairs.

She'd done all she could. It was up to him now.

Evangeline Jones knew exactly how to love hard and with no regrets.

She needed a man bold enough to do the same.

CHAPTER EIGHT

LOGAN couldn't get Evie out of his head. The long hours of travel couldn't shift her. The mountain of work that awaited him upon his return served only to make him more aware of how much he wanted her around *after* the day's work was done. One week after his return to London and he couldn't look at his bed without thinking of what Evie would look like in it. Passion-blind and soaring. Shiny-slick and smiling in the aftermath. He missed the brush of her shoulder against his as she cooked in her kitchen. Being in her space; having her invade his. He hadn't just tolerated it. He'd embraced it. A sucker for a soft touch, she'd teased him. Or a hard touch.

Any kind of touch as long as it was hers.

Only hers.

He didn't know what to do with a need so fierce and large. Didn't know how to make her a part of his life without demanding too much. Didn't know how to balance Evie's needs with his fear of one day losing control of his own desires and going too far. Of becoming possessive and controlling. Abusive. So many different ways to reach inside a person and tear them apart.

He'd texted her when he'd arrived back in London. 'Home,' he'd written.

And got a smiley face text in reply.

That was good, right? Not too needy or greedy on either side. Letting Evie get on with her life without him stomping all over it. Letting him get on with his.

No obsession here.

No overwhelming need to have her by his side.

Except that with each passing day Logan's need to hear Evie's voice and feel her touch grew stronger.

He lasted a week. One week before he rang his brother during Max's working day on the pretext of getting Max's opinion on converting an outer London warehouse into residential units. Max's speciality, not his. Was Max interested in taking on the project? Developing an international profile?

Was Evie?

'Since when have you been interested in redevelopment projects?' came his brother's guarded reply.

'Since staying with Evie in her warehouse apartment,' he countered. 'I didn't mind the experience.'

'Well, aren't you the lucky one?' said Max with unmistakeable bite. 'Did it ever occur to you that the reason you liked the warehouse apartment experience was because of the woman involved?'

'If you're not interested, all you have to do is say so,' countered Logan coolly.

Silence from Max's end. 'I'll talk it over with Evie,' he said grudgingly. 'I don't know that we're ready to take the company international. You looking to move on the warehouse fast?'

'Don't have to. Just letting you know it's there. Any news on the civic centre bid?'

'Looks promising,' said Max. 'There are three bids left on the table and one of them is ours.'

'Good,' said Logan. 'Good. What do you know about Sinclair House?'

'You mean Mum's latest charity? It's a safe house for victims of domestic abuse. She goes there once a fortnight and helps with meals or something. Why?'

'She hit me up for a donation. Apparently they need a new roof.' But Max's answer had piqued Logan's interest more than it had settled it. 'What do you mean she goes there once a fortnight?'

'Just what I said.'

'She needs to stop that. It's not safe.'

'It's a *safe* house, Logan. Heavy on the security windows and doors. Six-foot fences.'

'Yeah, and it's full of God knows who.'

'Mostly battered women and children, from what I can gather. What exactly do you think they're going to do?'

Logan shook his head. This was the difference between him and Max. Max had no goddamn idea what people were capable of. 'Desperate people do desperate things.'

'Yeah, and they also need help. What do you want me to do, Logan? Tell her to stop? That'd work on her almost as well as it works on you. *You* talk to her if you're that concerned about it. Heaven knows she treasures every last scrap of attention you throw her.'

'Hey, you're the favourite.'

'You know what? For all your legendary business acumen you're one blind son of a bitch.'

'Language, little brother.'

'Screw you. Don't start with me, Logan, or I'll serve

it straight back at you. Matter of fact I'm going to any-way. Why haven't you called Evie? Which, by the way, she predicted.'

'What do you mean *predicted*?'

'I mean when I asked her if she'd heard from you she said no, that wasn't part of the deal. What the *hell* kind of deal is that?'

'Look, Max—'

'Don't you "look, Max" me. You spend a week in-side a woman's skin, she opens up her home to you and her life to you and a week later you can't be bothered to give her five minutes of your precious time? What is *wrong* with you?'

'Nothing! I was just…giving her some space.' A gap-ing pit was beginning to form in Logan's stomach at the thought that something might have happened to her. 'Is she all right?'

'Evie's *fine*, Logan. Just *peachy*, thanks for asking. She does her work, she goes to the beach, she bought a Ducati road bike that goes from zero to one hundred in six point nine seconds, but don't let that alarm you. She's taking road-safety lessons from a former AMA Motocross champion called Duke, but don't let that bother you either. His manners are impeccable and he knows how to use a phone.'

'Hey, hold the PMS.'

'You deserve the PMS. You're treating a woman I respect and admire like a whore and she's letting you. Doesn't make it right.'

'If I'd wanted a sermon I'd have gone to church.'

'Go to hell, Logan. I vouched for you. I practically threw Evie at you, and *this* is how you repay me? By using her up and walking away without a backward

glance? *My* business partner. *My* friend. And your loss.
I'll give your regards to Duke.'

And then Max hung up on him.

'Who's Duke?' asked Evie as she strode into MEP's
outer office, head down and preoccupied, but not so
unconscious that she hadn't caught the way Max had
slapped his phone down on the desk, and there was
definitely no missing his scowl.

'Duke's the US motocross champion who's teach-
ing you how to ride your new Ducati,' said Max curtly.
'Don't ask.'

'Huh,' said Evie thoughtfully. 'Am I enjoying the
process?'

'Immensely.'

'Good for me,' she said. 'Because it's a good idea. I
take it that was Logan on the phone?'

Max nodded.

Evie smiled; she couldn't help it. 'So what else have
I been doing?'

'Not moping,' said Max. 'As a true friend I'm doing
my level best to ignore your current state of mope.'

'Excellent,' said Evie. 'Good for you too.'

'Do you remember how peaceful life was back in
the days before we got engaged and I made the idiotic
mistake of introducing you to my family?' Max asked
with a great deal of wistfulness. 'I do.'

'Never mind, Max. You'll fall in love yourself one
day, lose all sense of purpose, struggle mightily to keep
your life on track and probably fail miserably, but trust
me; I will be there to point it out to you. It'll be my
pleasure.'

'Must be catching,' said Logan.

'What?'

'PMS.'

'Just for that I'm not bringing you back any lunch.'

'I'll remember that when I'm rich and *you* want lunch. No champagne. No caviar. No lobster.'

'No problem. I've lived on tuna sandwiches before. I can do it again.'

'Maybe I should reassure Logan that you're not interested in his money,' said Max. 'Might help.'

'Tell him whatever the hell you like,' said Evie, doing an about turn and heading for the door. 'Maybe I could be flying fighter jets next time he calls. Stunt biplanes.'

'Get me a tuna sandwich,' Max called after her. 'And I won't tell him how much you're missing him.'

'Thank you.'

Evie heard the catch in her voice, but she kept on going because if she turned around and saw sympathy in Max's eyes, her carefully constructed world without Logan in it would probably come tumbling down. 'For that I'll bring you two.'

Logan called her that night, at her apartment rather than at work, and for that Evie was grateful. Eight-thirty p.m. her time and eleven-thirty a.m. in London. Middle of a businessman's day and she wondered where he was calling from, whether he'd squeezed her in between meetings, and most of all she clutched the phone and closed her eyes and concentrated on the sound of his voice saying her name. Some time soon she was going to have to speak, but not yet. Not until he said her name again.

Which he did.

'Hey,' she said. Best she could do—she was fresh out of amiable greetings.

'Max tells me you bought a Ducati.' Guess Logan was all out of pleasant small talk too.

'So I heard,' offered Evie.

'Which one?'

'The red one that goes really, really fast.' And there ended Evie's knowledge of motorbikes and her taste for silly lies. 'I didn't buy a Ducati, Logan. Your brother's messing with you.'

'He's not the only one.'

'Could be you bring it on yourself,' she murmured. 'Best guess.'

'I should have called you a week ago,' he said.

'Only if you wanted me to feel valued.' She let her comment hang for a moment, because she was nobody's pushover and he needed to know that. 'If, on the other hand, you were sorting out a few issues, like, say, the difference between wanting to stay in touch with someone and being so unhealthily obsessed with someone that you couldn't live without them... If a little bit of thinking time bought you some clarity on that issue... I'd call that time well spent.'

She could almost hear his brain churning.

'Generous of you,' he said finally, his voice sounding as if he'd just eaten a mile of gravel road.

'For you I can be generous.'

'So how've you been?' More gravel. Filler conversation.

'Okay.' Wasn't as if he was going to call her a liar. 'Work's been slow and I'm thinking of painting the ceiling of my apartment dark red.'

'Evangeline, parts of your ceiling are three storeys high.'

'I own half a construction company, Logan. There's this equipment called scaffolding.'

'I'm assuming you have people called employees as well?'

'So speaks the multimillionaire.' Evie rolled her eyes. 'I like painting. It's therapeutic. Besides, if you want something done right, do it yourself.'

'Don't say that,' he said with what Evie could have sworn was an underlying note of panic.

'Why not?'

'Because I've just created two new senior operations manager positions and filled them and I'm now on the hunt for a senior finance manager.'

'So…you're expanding?'

'Restructuring. I was causing bottlenecks. I needed to let go of some of the decision making. We'll see how it goes.'

'You don't sound convinced.'

'If you want something done right, do it yourself.'

'So I hear,' she said with a grin. 'Just think of all the bold *new* projects you'll be able to put your mark on before handing over the boring bits.'

'There is that,' he said. 'I want another week with you.'

'Before you hand over the boring bits?'

'You're not boring, Evangeline. You're challenging and wise and I'm a little bit terrified of you, but I wouldn't call you boring.'

'Would you call me submissive?'

A long pause from Logan; as if he knew he'd be judged on his answer. 'Not in general,' he said finally. 'Although on occasion you're willing to relinquish control to a more dominant sexual partner.'

'Good answer,' she said softly.

'Come to London, Evie. Come visit me. Same deal as I had with you. A hotel room for when and if you need it and an invitation to join me at my house should you so choose.'

'Logan—'

'Don't say no. It won't cost you anything but your time. First-class travel, with a stopover at, say, a landmark hotel in Dubai?'

'Are you serious?'

'Do you feel valued yet?'

'Remind me to tell you the difference between being valued and being bought.'

'Does that mean you *don't* want to experience the delights of a seven-star hotel?'

'Wash your mouth out,' she said. 'It could mean I never actually reach London.'

'*Now* who's feeling undervalued?'

'Hey, you started this,' she reminded him. 'Will you *join* me at the hotel in Dubai?'

'You don't like us together in hotel rooms, remember?'

'I'd like us in this one.'

'How does next week sound?'

'I can't do next week,' she said with a grimace she was glad Logan couldn't see. 'We'll know if we landed the civic centre job by Wednesday next week and I want to be here to either celebrate or commiserate.'

'Hnh.' Logan sounded ever so slightly annoyed.

'Don't people ever say no to you?' she murmured.

'People often say no to me,' he countered. 'My job is getting them to change their minds.'

'I'm not going to change my mind.'

'I know that, Evie. Hence the hnh. I'm just thinking ahead to what's coming up on *my* schedule that I can move around, that's all.'

'Oh.' It wouldn't hurt for her to give some credit to the pressures of *his* job while she was busy getting him to consider the challenges of hers. 'You'll be working through the day while I'm there, though, right? Same deal as when you were here and I went to work only this time I fit in around you?'

'You don't want to spend the entire week in Dubai?'

'No. One night should do it. On one condition.'

'What's that?'

'Promise you'll play tennis with me on the helipad.'

'Max, you're wearing out the floorboards,' said Evie. 'And you're driving me insane.' It was four-thirty on Wednesday afternoon and the reason that Max was driving her insane was that there was still no word on the civic centre bid. 'No news is good news.'

'I hate platitudes,' said Max. 'We didn't get it. We almost got married for nothing.'

'You almost got married?' asked a startled Carlo, who was hovering there with them, waiting on that call. Jeremy was there too—a junior site engineer who'd been with them for two years. So was Kit, one of their electrical subcontractors. Nervous people with nothing to do but wait on a phone call that hadn't yet come.

'It's a long story,' said Evie. 'Max wanted to marry me for his money but wiser heads prevailed. Besides… that was before I met his big brother.'

'Impressive?' asked Kit.

'Be still my beating heart.'

'Evie, one more platitude out of you and violence will ensue,' threatened Max. 'C'mon phone. *Ring.*'

'A watched pot never boils,' said Kit.

'I thought it was "kettle",' offered Jeremy. 'A watched kettle never—'

And then the phone rang and shut them all up.

Suddenly it wasn't so much fun to tease Max any more. He'd thrown everything he had at this job and if they didn't get it he was going to be gutted. Carlo headed for his office cubicle, taking Jeremy with him. Kit eyed Max warily and then said, 'Got any biscuits in the tea room?' and took himself off.

Evie debated heading for her office but Max grabbed her by the wrist and mouthed 'Stay,' as he listened intently to whatever the person on the other end of that phone was saying.

Max let her wrist go when she nodded, and then Evie sat on the edge of the table and tucked her hands beneath her legs and waited. Max resumed his pacing. Evie most definitely wanted to land this job. But her heart wasn't in it the way Max's was.

'Yes,' said Max, and, 'yes,' again. All very restrained.

The smile that swept across his handsome features moments later was not so restrained. Max's smile thought it was Christmas and there was a pony under the tree.

He laughed and said he was looking forward to it. He set up a meeting for tomorrow morning. And then he got the hell off the phone.

'We got it,' he said. 'We got it!'

'Of course we did,' said Evie as Max swept her up into a bear hug and swung her around. 'MEP's architect is a visionary, the company's on its way up and the price was right. What time is it in London?'

'Ah, early morning? Seven-thirty? You calling Logan?'

'Texting him, to be safe. I'm telling him we're about to spend his money.'

'So…you're talking again?' asked Max. 'There's been contact?'

'There has. And I didn't have to instigate it.'

'That's good,' said Max. 'That's very good.' He squeezed her once more before releasing her. 'Kit,' he bellowed. 'Break out the beer.'

The party started at the office and moved to the local bar, where there was more food and a better beverage selection than the one they had at the office. Their concreter turned up with a few of his crew—nothing like the promise of more work and free drinks to raise a man's spirits. Evie's spirits too, and who cared if she got ribbed for drinking champagne rather than beer? Not her problem if her co-workers preferred beer. Not her job to tell them to cease with the swearing, although she had a feeling that most of them *did* try to curb their language around her, which boggled the mind given the curses that still slipped through.

'How about asking Juliet Grace to come and be our new project manager?' she said as Max reached past her to put his empty beer glass down and pick up a handful of peanuts. 'She's detail oriented, most of us know her, or know of her, and she can handle this lot.'

'A woman.' Max eyed her dubiously.

'Careful, Max. Your biases are showing.'

'I'm not biased. I'm thinking.'

Evie laughed; she couldn't help it. 'Do you think more beer will help?'

Logan stood outside the busy Sydney bar and watched as the slim woman with the raven-black hair and wicked smile signalled the barman for another round of drinks. Max stood with her and so did at least a dozen other men. Labourers half of them, they looked as if they'd come straight from a job. A tight-knit group, intent on celebration, and it was clear that Evie was one of them. Accepted by them. Protected by them, even if she didn't know it.

Though she probably did.

Evie had texted him that they'd won the contract. That particular message had been waiting for him when he'd got off the plane in Sydney.

He should have texted Evie back. Should have said, 'I'm in Sydney. Where are you?'

But uncertainty was riding him hard this evening and he'd texted Max instead.

It didn't look as if Max had told Evie that Logan was on his way. She didn't look like a woman who was waiting for her lover to walk through the door. Evangeline Jones had a very fine habit of extracting pleasure from the moment—no angst-ing required.

Logan envied her.

The amount of anguish that had gone into Logan's decision to get on a plane so that he could be with Evie and Max come civic centre decision time could have filled the Pacific. Would Evie find it presumptuous? Would Max? Would they want him there?

All he knew was that for the first time in his life he was reaching out and wanting to be a part of something, as opposed to keeping everything and everyone at arm's length.

Arm's length being the distance whereby he couldn't inadvertently hurt anyone and they couldn't hurt him.

Logan watched as some moron bumped Evie in the shoulder as he turned away from the bar with a tray full of drinks in hand. He watched as Max automatically slung his arm around Evie's shoulder and drew her to his side.

Logan didn't viciously resent Evie and Max's camaraderie. He didn't catch his breath and look down at the concrete beneath his feet in an attempt to manage that part of him that wanted to take Max apart, piece by bloody piece, for daring to touch what was his. Not him.

He looked back and tried to *not* want to beat his brother bloody.

Nope. Still no luck letting go of that particular desire.

He was so screwed.

Logan watched as Evie moved out from beneath Max's shoulder and settled herself on a barstool. Men at her back and beside her and the table beneath her elbow now. Protected on all fronts. Also hogging the peanuts.

What if she didn't *want* to make room for Logan in her life tonight?

Because it was one thing for Max to know that Logan and Evie were tangling. It was quite another to walk in there and stake his claim on her in front of people she had to work with. God knew he had no desire to undermine her authority.

Maybe if he *didn't* stake his claim—just went in there and kept his hands and his mouth off her…

Be Max's brother rather than Evie's lover. Keep everything casual and easy—no biting jealousy or had-to-see-you-again obsession here. If he could do that...

It was a pretty big if.

Moments later Logan's phone beeped.

'What the hell are you doing?' the message from his brother read, and he looked up and his brother was fiddling with his phone and Evie was deep in laughing conversation with the giant across the table from her.

Another text from Max. 'You want a gold-plated invitation?'

The short answer being yes. Either that or a machete to cut through the mess of thoughts and feelings roiling round inside him.

With a shake of his head, Logan pocketed his phone and headed for the open doorway of the bar. He'd know soon enough if he'd done the right thing by coming here.

And he'd take her dismay straight up, if that was what she served him.

The noise level was high as Logan stepped inside. The smell of hops permeated the air. Not exactly an upscale establishment, this one. Cheerful though. And then Max lifted his arm and gestured him over and bent to whisper something in Evie's ear and she whipped around and the smile that lit her face wrapped around Logan's heart and wouldn't let go.

Her smile said she didn't consider his presence an intrusion.

Her smile telegraphed a message Logan had waited a lifetime to hear.

Pleasure—not pain—because he was near.

Max snagged Evie's champagne glass from her as she pushed through the circle of men and headed straight for him and then she was in his arms and her lips were on his and she tasted of strawberries and champagne and generous, genuine welcome.

If ever there was a time to keep his wits about him this was it, but the kiss deepened anyway, capturing him so completely that there was no room for anything else. Only Evie.

Wolf whistles helped him to remember where he was.

Evie's reckless smile told him she knew exactly where she was and that she didn't mind laying claim to him in public in the slightest. She brushed her thumb over his lips and kissed him swiftly once more, and then took him by the arm and propelled him forward towards the group she'd been sitting with.

'Everyone, this is Logan Black. He bankrolls us from time to time. He's also Max's brother.'

Max picked up two drinks from the table—a whisky shot and a beer chaser. 'You're going to have to catch up,' he said, and handed them to Logan.

Max's casual welcome worked to soothe Logan some. The welcome said, 'I know damn well you've never been this invested in my successes before, but I'm open to it no matter what the reason. You're my brother. You want in, you're in.'

'Doesn't seem entirely wise,' said Logan, but he took the drinks anyway, sent the whisky straight down and set the beer on the table for later. 'Congratulations on landing the job.'

'Thanks.' Max clasped Logan's forearm to his. 'Couldn't have done it without you. You just get in?'

'Yeah.'

'You *knew* he was coming in?' asked Evie.

'Surprise,' said Max and grinned, warm and wide,

at Evie's narrow-eyed glare. 'Who says I can't keep a secret?'

'It was very last-minute,' Logan offered by way of lame excuse. 'Didn't know if I'd make it in time.'

'You came straight from the plane?'

Logan rubbed ruefully at his bristly jaw—he'd last shaved back in London, about thirty hours ago by his count. 'Why? Does it show?'

'To your extreme advantage,' said Evie dryly. 'You are so *pretty* when you get all tousled and unshaven. Have you eaten?'

'No.'

'Most of this lot will clear out in another hour or so. I was planning on grabbing a meal somewhere nearby with your brother. Which should in no way be construed as a date,' she added with a touch of anxiety.

'I'll keep that in mind.' He liked that little hint of anxiousness in her. He liked it a lot. And hated himself for it. His father had kept his mother anxious, always one breath away from outright fear. God, he remembered her fear. This wasn't the same.

Dear God, make it not be the same.

'You want to come along?' she asked next.

'Yeah.' Logan ran a hand through his hair and looked to the bar rather than at Evie.

'Yeah, that'd be good,' he muttered.

'What's good?' asked Max.

'Food.'

'When?'

'Whenever you're done here.'

He wasn't jealous of the bond Evie shared with Max. He *wasn't*.

'One more round,' said Max and Logan nodded.

'Max's happy,' he said as his brother turned away.

'Very,' replied Evie. 'There'll be no living with him after this. He's going to drive the workmen on this project bonkers. Fortunately, I have a solution. Her name's Juliet Grace.'

'She's going to distract him?'

'Not at all. Juliet's a construction manager with forty years' worth of high-end project management under her belt.' Evie smiled sagely. 'She's going to control him.'

Evie made Logan feel wanted. There was no other explanation for the warmth in his body and the smile that came so readily to his lips. Easy to make an effort to fit in when a person felt wanted. Cost him nothing to satisfy people's curiosity about what he did for a living and to grin and wear it when one of them asked him where he'd been all Evie's life. 'He's mine,' Evie told them more than once. 'All mine. I saw him first.'

'But I have a puppy,' called Kit. 'I bet Logan likes puppies.'

'I have goldfish,' said another pure soul.

'I have breasts,' said Evie smugly and Logan almost choked on his beer as Kit pouted and the men around him roared. She knew how to handle her subbies, damned if she didn't.

'Max, you got another brother?' asked Kit.

Max shook his head and met Logan's gaze with an affectionate one of his own. 'One's enough.'

'Cousin?' asked Kit, and Max glanced back at Kit with a quick grin.

'She's married.'

'Guess you'll have to do,' said Kit with a devil's slow grin.

And Max blushed.

Logan leaned in towards Evie and she made it easy for him by tucking into the circle of his arms. 'Did my brother just blush?' he whispered in her ear.

'You're very astute.'

'Are they—?' Shock robbed him of words.

'Not yet.'

'But has he *ever*—?' Still no words.

'You mean has *Max* ever? Not that I know of, but it wouldn't surprise me. Kit's not the type to persist when he knows the other guy's straight. And he *has* been persisting. Which means Max hasn't yet given him a definitive no.'

'Who is this Kit?' he wanted to know. 'What does he do?'

'Protective,' murmured Evie and wove her fingers through his. 'I like that. Kit's an electrician. Runs his own company. Subcontracts on big commercial jobs, mainly. Shopping centres. Stadiums. High rises. Jobs that are worth his while. Subcontracts for us every so often on jobs that aren't always worth his while.'

'Fancy that.'

'Yes, he does.'

Logan looked from his brother to the tanned, blue-eyed blond called Kit, who'd abandoned his pursuit of Max in favour of watching football on the big screen. Was Max *really* falling for this man? Did that mean he was reassessing his sexual preferences? Or had he always been looking in that direction and Logan had just never noticed? God! Logan was going to have to rethink every last memory of his brother that he had. 'How did I *miss* this? I need to get home more.'

'Your brother thinks the world of you, Logan,' said

Evie, and there was something approaching seriousness in her voice. 'Wouldn't hurt.'

Logan watched the game on the big screen for a moment or two before turning his attention back to the man who apparently had a puppy and wasn't afraid to use it. 'Hey, Kit. What's the score?'

'Nil all.' Kit shot them a darkly amused glance. 'I'll let you know if anyone scores.'

Evie grinned.

'Next time, *warn* me,' muttered Logan.

'Next time, *call* me when you're coming to visit,' countered Evie. 'And I will. They've been circling one another all week. Best show in town. Mind you, that's what Max says about us.'

'Evangeline, do you and Max have *any* distance between you whatsoever when it comes to your personal lives?'

'Some.' Evie held up her forefinger and thumb an inch or so apart and turned her head so that she could see his eyes. 'We're friends who work together. We're in each other's face all day and we know what's going on in each other's lives. There's no lust. It shouldn't bother you.' Apparently she could see that it did. 'You shouldn't let it bother you,' she said firmly, and brought his hand up to her lips and pressed a quick kiss to the knuckle of his thumb.

Eventually, the MEP crowd thinned. Max kept smiling but seemed somewhat preoccupied. The swaggering Kit had ambled over to the snooker tables in the far corner of the room and started playing. Money was changing hands. Kit looked as if he was working towards finding trouble. Logan eyed the rest of the sharks over by the pool tables. He wouldn't have to wait long.

'Ready to go find something to eat?' Max asked them, with a swift glance in Kit's direction.

'Your call,' said Logan, for it was Max's party. 'He coming too?'

Max shot him a sharp glance.

Logan shrugged and raised an eyebrow. Acknowledgement, if that was what his brother wanted. An innocent question if not.

'I—ah.' Max glanced Kit's way again and this time the other man turned around and caught his eye. Long glances were exchanged before Max turned away. 'No. I don't know what I'm doing there. Probably not a good idea to do it in front of you two.'

'Stay here, then,' offered Logan. 'See if your pool-hustling friend wants to grab a bite to eat with just you and then stumble around all you want. Who's going to see?'

Max laughed tightly. '*He'll* see. Lord, I've got no experience with this. *None.*'

'Chances are Kit knows that,' offered Evie.

'You don't mind?' asked Max gruffly, and his question wasn't just for Evie. Max was looking at Logan with something that looked a lot like pleading.

'It's your call,' he said again, not knowing what other assurances to give his brother, and hell would freeze over before he started dishing out advice. 'I'll run with whatever you want.'

Max glanced back towards Kit again, and that was enough for Logan. 'We're going. You're staying. Not sure I ever want details.'

'Amen to that,' said Max and with a wry nod he headed towards Kit.

Evie tucked in beside Logan as they left the pub. She

put her hand in the crook of his arm and every time her shoulder brushed his Logan felt tension leave his body. It was the most relaxed Logan had felt in over a week. 'What do you want to eat?' she asked him.

'Thai?'

'Perfect.'

Even the way she said *perfect* was perfect. Evie embraced the *now* better than anyone else he knew.

'Damn, I'm glad you're here,' she said, bumping his arm this time and making Logan grin. 'What brings you here? Apart from me.'

Cocky. Entitled. And damned if he didn't love that about her too.

'I came because of Max too. I just wanted to be here when the civic centre decision came through.'

'Good for you,' she said. 'Good for me. How long can you stay?'

'I have a morning flight to Perth. I need to be back in London in three days' time.'

Evie stopped abruptly. '*One* day? Not even that?'

'Work's a little crazy right now. I'm sorting it.'

'Why didn't you say so earlier?' Evie's hands were on her hips, her eyes telegraphing irritation. 'We could have left that pub an hour ago. You could have been in my bed by now. Where's your brain?'

Nowhere close by.

There was a shadowy shopfront doorway just a few steps away and Logan took full advantage of it, pulling Evie into the darkness along with him and backing her up against the wall. He'd been holding back all evening, knowing that the eyes of people she worked with were on them. Never undermine the boss's authority. Golden rule of business, so he'd packed his need to stake his claim on her away and kept his hands and his mouth to himself for the most part.

But there were no work colleagues watching them now.

Threading his fingers through hers, Logan brought Evie's hands above her head and leaned in to capture her lips in a kiss so deeply consuming that he feared he might forget his own name.

Though there'd be no forgetting hers.

Evie moaned, deep down in her chest, and her fingers closed tightly over his.

A gasp from Evie as he moved on from her mouth and set tongue to that little V between shoulder and neck. A whimper from him as her body arched in search of his. Hands at her waist now, gathering her close.

'Logan, please. Let me take you home,' she whispered, with her hands in his hair and her mouth to his temple. 'Please, before I come apart. There's food in the fridge, I can feed you if you're hungry, just—the things I want to do to you—I don't want an audience. Just you.'

Logan groaned and loosened his hold. 'Hire-car keys are in my front pocket,' he told her and groaned anew when she found them. 'I swear the car's around here somewhere. Back the other way.'

So they went back the other way and found the car and Evie drove them home. He didn't touch her until the door of her apartment shut behind her. He didn't dare. And then he dropped his overnight case by the door and looked at her and then she was in his arms and sanctuary was his along with salvation.

He didn't want to have to take control tonight; he'd never be able to maintain it. But she didn't ask it of him, just got busy with the removal of his clothes until it was skin on skin and hunger driving them, no room for any other edges between them this time.

Too many stairs to make it to the bedroom and the sofa was right there, soft and wide and the cushions could go and he could be on his back with Evie sliding over him, right there, for ever there.

Owning him heart and soul.

CHAPTER NINE

LOGAN left before dawn. 'Got to be in Perth this morning,' he whispered against her lips and Evie opened sleep-heavy eyes and smiled, because although he was dressed in a business suit and tie, the conventional clothes, he still had sex god stamped all over him as far as she was concerned.

'Do come again,' she murmured and fell back asleep in the time it took him to cross the floor and reach the stairs.

When she woke again, she woke alone, but the memory of last night stayed with her. Of Logan's acute pleasure and her own, and the memory made her stretch lazily and smile and roll over into his side of the bed just so that she could close her eyes and breathe in the scent of him on her sheets. She scrubbed her face against the pillow, ran her hand over the not-so-smooth-any-more sheets.

'Morning,' she murmured. Wherever he was.

And she wondered how long it would take him this time, before he returned to her again.

Easy enough to give a man his freedom if Evie's heart weren't truly in it and they were simply travelling the friends-with-benefits road, but that wasn't the road they were on, she and Logan.

And it was getting ever more difficult to let him go with a smile and pretend that she wasn't totally lost in him, more so now than she had ever been.

New day. A working day—at least she still had that. Not to mention a project that would keep her on her toes for the next eight months. There were management tiers to put in place. Checks and double checks when it came to the quality of the work. There were plenty of things to be going on with.

Where did Logan say he was going to be today?

Running her hand up under Logan's pillow, she felt the jab of something pointed and hard. She pushed the pillow aside and curled her hand around the brightly co-loured paper thing and brought it in for closer inspec-tion. Her lips curved when she finally recognised what it was: a folded-up paper parasol, the kind they put in cocktails. She'd asked for one once.

And Logan had remembered.

Evie rolled over on her back and popped the para-sol and twirled it between her fingers before tucking it behind her ear.

Time to be grateful for the richness of life and the moments of sheer joy to be found in it. Like last night, when she'd first spotted Logan in the pub. There could be no hellos like that without a goodbye. As of last night she was very fond of Logan's hellos.

'Atta girl, Evie,' she whispered by way of a pep talk. 'Concentrate on those.'

There were five more hellos over the next two and a half months. Evie never got to go to Dubai or to London, for both she and Max had underestimated the management required to take on a big job and expand the business at the same time. Their bad; and the only way to fix it was to work their butts off and pray that the people they currently had in place would hold. Kit had been worth his weight in gold. If Max didn't make Kit family soon, Evie was tempted to do it for him.

Of those five hellos, four had been weekend stints where Logan had come to visit her. Once, Evie had spent the weekend with him in Perth. He owned an apartment there, and it was spacious and expensively furnished but it wasn't his home.

She hoped it wasn't his home for there'd been nothing of Logan in it. It had been a corporate executive's landing pad—a serviced apartment, one step up from a hotel suite. Logan had a real home tucked away somewhere. Some place that allowed him to refresh and renew.

Didn't he?

So there was sex, which ran the gamut from incandescently reverent to edgy to needy and greedy.

And there was work, and Logan knew so much more about hers than she did about his. Max had asked Logan's advice when it came to company expansion and Logan had given it, although not without fair warning that he was more used to stripping a company than growing one. He'd helped them keep the company structure lean, flexible, and Evie appreciated his input, she really did.

But their love life and her working life were becoming so entangled now. Logan being Max's brother. Logan and Max growing closer and closer and Evie loved watching that particular bond strengthen, she *did*.

So what if she woke up way too early some mornings thinking that if she lost Logan she would somehow lose everything else as well?

Too entwined for comfort. No reassurances as to where they were headed with this relationship and it made Evie jumpy and ultra-sensitive to criticism and, dear heaven, did she mention moody?

When Logan was around life couldn't be finer.

But when he left he did it with as little fanfare as possible and he never, *ever* said when he'd return.

Evie knew the why of it. She'd *known* it would be like this.

But the uncertainty was soul-grinding and the road they were travelling was a hard one and Evie was acutely aware that she'd promised Logan that she'd known where they were going with this. That she would be able to show him the way.

Fine words.

And not an ounce of common sense in sight.

'Lover boy still ignoring you?' asked Kit as he disassembled the last piece of scaffolding in Evie's living room and set about packing up his tools. He looked up at the blood-red ceiling and shook his head.

'Looks good, doesn't it?' said Evie.

'Gonna have to call you Mistress Dread.'

Kit had been coming around to her place on and off for a couple of weeks now—a result of Max still jerking him around and of Evie genuinely liking the man. They'd had enough in common for friendship to fall easily into place. Work ties. Mutual friends. Dysfunctional love lives…

'How long has it been since he last remembered your existence?' asked Kit again.

'Three weeks.' Three weeks since he'd last graced her with his presence.

'Train wreck.' Kit dropped his carry case by the door and followed her into the kitchen. 'How long you going to keep indulging him?'

'Says he whose boyfriend won't even acknowledge him.'

'That's different,' said Kit with impressive complacency.

'Yeah, because Maxxie's a *special* snowflake,' muttered Evie as she headed for the fridge, pulled out a beer and waved it at Kit, who nodded and took it from her before settling back against the bench, relaxed and easy in her company and looking decidedly more angelic than tragic. Sunlight streaming through the window and landing on blond hair, broad shoulders and blue eyes did that.

'Max has got a lot to come to grips with,' offered Kit. 'Social issues. Personal expectations. What's Logan's excuse? He doesn't even call you.'

'Logan's a busy man.'

'No one's that busy, Evie. It's a power play.'

'No, it's his safety check. It shows that he's still in control of his feelings for me. That he's not obsessed or demanding or—'

'In love,' said Kit.

'That too.' Evie offered up a tired smile. 'That's the last thing Logan wants to be.'

Kit said nothing.

'You think I should cut him loose?'

'It's an option.'

'Would you cut Max loose?'

'Thinking about it,' said Kit, and Evie choked on the water she'd just put to her lips.

'Seriously?'

Kit shrugged. 'If Max can't resolve his issues about being with me, then, yeah. Why stick around?'

'You don't mean that.'

But Kit just shrugged and set the beer to his lips. Maybe he did.

'How much longer are you going to give him?' she asked cautiously.

'That's the million-dollar question.'

'He relies on you,' offered Evie. 'He gets less stressed about the work when he knows you're coming in.'

Kit just looked at her.

'Maybe you could take a fall from a roof one day, land in hospital and see if Max comes running?' she said. 'That might work.'

'Maybe you could get pregnant with Logan's baby,' said Kit by way of reply. 'I hear that one works too.'

Evie grimaced. 'What else we got?'

'How about making Logan jealous? Bring on the other man.'

'For that Logan would have to actually be present,' said Evie. 'But I could definitely see the other man working for you. Maybe it's time for you to introduce Max to a former lover. One who relishes his extremely good life and the part you once played in it. One who still values you. Got any of those?'

'One or two.'

'I thought you might. That was a compliment, by the way. I can see why people wouldn't want to let you go completely. You're handy.' Evie gestured towards the scaffolding. 'Helpful. Pretty. And smart.'

'Please, my ego, it swells.'

'Nothing but the truth,' said Evie. 'Besides, ego is good for you. It smacks of self-esteem. I had self-esteem too, once. I had a handle on my world. Didn't spend half my life staring at the phone that never rings.' Evie traced a water trail across the counter to the ring that showed where the jug of water she'd taken from the fridge had once been.

'Evie, if it's that bad, let him go.'

'I know,' she said, but her voice lacked conviction. 'Thing is, parts of my relationship with Logan work just *fine*.'

'You mean the sex is hotter than the sun.'

That was exactly what she meant. 'I swear, all he has to do is—'

'Evie!' Nothing like a little panic from a houseguest. 'Too much information.'

'I was going to say "look at me and I'm his",' she finished dryly.

'Ah,' said Kit. 'Well, now I know that. Continue.'

'I was hoping for a little more control over my desire for Logan by now, but it's not happening.'

'That's because he keeps you hungry for him. Always leaves you wanting just that little bit more. You need to gorge on him. Get him out of your system.'

'You really think that'll fix it?'

'No, but you'll have fun.'

'You are *not* helpful. I take it back.'

'Seriously, Evie. If you want my advice, it's to stop letting Logan pick you up and put you down as he pleases. If you want to call him, call him. If you want to see him, tell him you're on your way and expect him to welcome you. Take a little more control over this relationship. Don't keep making excuses for him.'

'You think I've lost control?'

Kit gave her the look he usually reserved for brain-dead sheep. 'Evie, you only have to look at the man and you're his. Your words, not mine. Did you ever have it?'

Later that evening—evening for her, Saturday morning for Logan—Evie picked up the phone and dialled Logan's London number. If you want contact, make contact. Step one in Evie's new and improved plan for surviving a long-distance relationship with a busy, busy man.

'I have a red ceiling,' she said when he answered the phone, his voice all gravelly and sleep heavy. 'It's kind of sexy.'

'Fits,' he mumbled.

'Did I wake you?'

'No.'

'Liar.'

'Maybe.' She could hear the smile in his voice. 'Late night last night.'

'Party?'

'Work. Two buyers looking at mining rights I hold in NSW.'

'You're into mining?'

'Sometimes I end up with mining assets as part of a broader transaction. Occasionally I'll keep them a while and bundle them before on selling but usually I spin them off fast. Miners get to keep their jobs if I can turn them over fast.'

'You're all heart.'

'Tell me about it. Did you want something, Evie?'

'Just to catch up.' Evie really should have gone into this conversation with a plan. He sounded marginally more awake. 'See what you've been doing. That sort of thing.'

'Work,' he said.

'Dull boy.'

Logan grunted his agreement. Or maybe it was disagreement.

'You haven't called me in three weeks,' she said. 'Why is that? And don't say work.'

'Getting pretty bossy there, Evie.'

'I prefer to call it frustrated. Sexually. Emotionally. Categorically. And that's another thing. No more leaving here without waking me. I hate it.'

'I figured it for a courtesy,' he offered warily.

'It's a cop-out. You lay me bare and yourself right along with me and then you sneak away like a thief because you don't want to deal with the fallout.'

'You really want to do this over the phone?' No mistaking the edge of ice in his voice.

'No. I'd much rather fight with you when you're here,' she said sweetly. 'But you're *not*.'

'So...You want to see me?'

'*Yes*, Logan. Yes.'

'So you can fight with me.'

'*Yes.*'

'And then what?'

'Wild make-up sex? Just a thought.'

'God, Evie!' Well, at least now he was fully awake. 'You don't think the sex gets wild enough?'

'I *do* think the sex gets wild enough. The sex is out of this world. You *know* that, Logan. I'd just happen to like more of it. More of everything.'

'We live on different continents. It's not an easy fix. I come when I can and I distinctly remember inviting you here months ago. How many times have you been?'

The answer to that being none.

The excuses for that being flimsy indeed.

'I'm not the only one who gets caught up in their work,' argued Logan. 'I've respected that. I haven't badgered you to come and visit me. I haven't pushed plane tickets on you. I've backed away from doing anything that could be construed as an affront to your independence. You live a full and satisfying life and you make sure I know it. I've been waiting for you to step into my life—take *one* step towards knowing more about me—but you don't. So don't you beat on me for being the only one who keeps their distance in this relationship, Evangeline. You do it too.'

Evie hated hearing the tight anger in Logan's voice. She hated even more that he was right.

'I can be in London next weekend,' she offered in a smaller voice than she would have liked. 'Get in on the Friday, leave on the Tuesday, maybe. Would that suit?'

'Yes.' He waited a beat. 'I promised you Dubai.'

'I don't want Dubai.' Evie was pretty sure this wasn't what Kit meant when he suggested she take a little more control of her relationship with Logan. 'I want you.'

'Evie.' She could hear the breath he took. The way it shook. 'I know I'm no good at relationships. Building them. Maintaining them. I don't even know the way. I try not to take too much. It's important to me that I don't try to manipulate you. Go all needy on you. It's essential to me that you have enough room to breathe.'

'Logan, you're not your father.' A bold statement on

Evie's part, because they *never* talked about his father. Not since that first time.

But her comment only got her a whole lot of silence in reply. 'Logan?'

'I can be like him though,' he said finally.

'When? When have you *ever* been like him?'

'In my head. Sometimes the things I want from you...'

'What things?' she asked quietly, and when he didn't answer immediately, 'Logan, what things?'

'Your attention.' His voice had gone rough. 'I crave it. More of it. Your eyes on me. Your hands on me. When you smile for me. All of it.'

'That's not so bad,' she whispered as desire pooled deep in her belly. 'Can't you see I've just asked the same of you? We've both been holding back. It's okay to want more. We can do more without tipping over into obsession and we'll both feel more content. You'll see.'

'Want you to myself sometimes,' he said next. 'Want everything and everyone else to get the hell out of my way.'

'That can be arranged, sometimes,' she murmured. 'It's not unusual for lovers to want privacy. Balance, Logan. We just have to find the right balance.'

'Sometimes I can't find it,' he murmured.

'We can deal with it.'

'Your body, for example. It's mine.'

'Yes.' No argument with him there. 'It is.'

CHAPTER TEN

Evie made what they were doing sound so easy. She made it sound like the normal give and take that occurred within a relationship. Her needs and his; explored and explained away. Some needs indulged; no recriminations and no dismay. He'd put her front and centre of a corporate negotiation team any day, fully confident that she would return with the deal she wanted and a couple of souls besides.

Lord knew she had her fingers well and truly wrapped around his.

Seven-thirty on a chilly winter's night and Logan stood waiting by the arrival doors for the passengers from Sydney-Singapore to trickle through.

'I could get used to first-class travel,' Evie had texted him from Singapore, and if Logan had his way she would. Evie had paid for her own airfare; she'd insisted. And then Logan had had her bumped up to first. She needed to indulge him in this, he'd told her simply. This was normal give and take.

No denying that Logan was nervous when Evie finally reached him, trailing luggage-on-wheels behind her. Easy enough to take her in his arms and hold her close and smile as his lips brushed her hair. Smile some more when her lips met his, warm and full of promise.

'Good trip?' he asked her as they headed for his car.

'I slept,' she said with an air of deep satisfaction. 'On the plane—on this lay-back seat-bed chair thingy. First time for everything.'

'Glad to hear it.' She had a smile that could light up his world. A skip in her stride that spoke of enjoyment and anticipation. 'And glad you could make it.'

Evie sobered a little at this. 'Me too,' she said quietly.

The drive back to Logan's penthouse apartment at Imperial Wharf took time. Friday night, couldn't be helped, but they got there eventually and the porter let them in and bade them good evening and Evie nodded in some bemusement.

'You have a porter?' she whispered as the door closed behind him.

'The complex does.' Logan guided her to the lift. The eighth, ninth and tenth floors were his. The apartment was far too big for one person, but he could afford it and he liked living close to the Thames. He watched for Evie's reaction from the corner of his eye as he led her through the entrance hall and into the reception room with its three-storey-high floor-to-ceiling windows and one-hundred-and-eighty-degree views. Nothing wrong with his apartment, he'd paid good money for it, but he wanted her to like it and, by the look of her, she did.

'Wow,' she murmured. 'This is *gorgeous*. Max would be proud.'

'The architect of the family has already given it his seal of approval,' murmured Logan. 'Though he doesn't think much of the interior decoration.'

'It's very…white,' she said with a grin. 'I'll bring you some paint.'

'Keep your paint,' said Logan. 'I like white. Off white. Nearly white. Possibly white. Besides, not all of the rooms are white. Some of them are taupe. And the wallpaper in the master bedroom is stripy grey. You'll like it.'

'Oh, you poor love.' She stood in place and turned a slow circle. 'It really is gorgeous. I'm looking for a personal touch.'

'Yeah. Keep looking.' Evie would find no family treasures here. No photos. No favourite childhood things.

He'd left them all behind.

He collected old maps but they weren't displayed on walls. He had his favourite bath scrub and aftershave but the rest he left up to the housekeeper who came in three times a week and cooked for him and filled his fridge because she complained she had nothing to do for all the mark he left on the place.

And then Evie turned around and caught him watching her and he acknowledged the fact with a half-smile and a shrug.

'Not a lot of you in here, is there?' she murmured.

'No.' He pushed away from the doorway he'd been leaning against. 'But it's private, the fridge is full and it's quiet. I can relax here.'

'I'll take your word for it,' she murmured dulcetly. 'I can probably relax here too. May I have the tour?'

Eight bedrooms, two kitchens, two cloakrooms, a cinema room, an office, various bathrooms and a roof-top summerhouse later, Evie draped her crimson velvet coat over a nearby chair, slumped down on a pale-grey suede lounge and said, 'Enough. You can draw me a map later.'

'Have you eaten?' The fridge was full, no need to go out.

'Yes.'

'Get you a drink?' he asked next.

'No, thank you,' she said, eyes closed as she leaned her head back against the low, puffy pillows. 'I don't need anything at the moment.' One eye popped open as if reconsidering. She patted the cushion beside her and Logan watched as the pat turned into a caress as Evie's fingers moved over the pale suede. 'There's room for you.'

And then her phone rang and she got up and fished it out of her coat pocket and frowned. 'It's your brother,' she said, before putting the phone to her ear. 'Hey, Max. This better not be about the work I left on your desk. Because I left it on your desk for a reason.'

But Evie's smile faded fast as she listened to Max's reply, and her eyes cut to Logan. 'Yes, he's here. No, he's not driving. We just got in.' Moments later Evie held the phone out towards Logan. 'He wants to talk to you.'

Puzzled, Logan took it and put it to his ear. No need for introductions, he already knew who it was. 'What?'

'Hey.' One word and Logan knew something was wrong. The tone wasn't right. Tension ran through the phone line like a living thing. 'It's Mum. She's been taken to hospital. They're operating on her now.'

'What happened?' Logan had a love-hate relationship with his mother. It had been that way for a long time. But an icy prickle started at his scalp and swept down over his body leaving dread in its wake.

'I don't know,' offered Max tightly. 'Some kind of

incident at the shelter she volunteers at. The one for battered women and kids. A fight.'

'A *what*?'

Evie had come to stand beside him, her hand resting on the curve of his stomach, nothing sexual about it, just touch, soft and gentle. Keeping him upright. Stopping his guts from spilling out.

'They're saying she took a blow to the head. Logan—' Max's voice cracked. 'It's bad. I need you here. She needs you here. Can you come?'

'I'll come.' Halfway across the world and unable to even *get* there for at least twenty-four hours. More like thirty-six. And Evie was here. Evie, who'd just flown twenty-four hours to get here. 'I'll be there. Soon as I can.'

'I'll keep in touch,' said Max and hung up.

And Logan just stood there, his mind blank.

'Logan.'

A soft voice penetrated the fog that was his brain. Evie's voice, and she took the phone from him and pocketed it and then her hands were on him again, firmer this time, one to his chest, the other rubbing gently back and forth along his upper arm. 'What's going on?'

'My mother's in surgery.'

'And Max wants you there?'

Logan nodded. 'I'm sorry. The weekend. I can't—'

'All right,' said Evie soothingly. 'Hey, Logan. Easy.' Evie wasn't the one who was swaying, he realised belatedly. He was.

'A few clothes in a travel bag. That's all you need,' Evie was saying next. 'I'm already packed.'

'You can't want to—

'Get on the next plane home?' she finished for him.

'Yeah, I can. C'mon, Logan, I can't remember where your bedroom is. You're going to have to help me out here.'

The man was in shock. No way could Logan drive back to the airport in his condition. Evie got him to his bedroom. She found a travel bag in his dressing room and shoved it on the rack in there and left him to it while she went in search of the porter. Evie had only the vaguest idea of what a porter manning the door of a swanky apartment complex actually did.

What she *needed* him to do was magic a taxi to the door within the next five minutes.

He didn't disappoint.

Thirty hours later Evie and Logan strode into the waiting room outside Intensive Care. They'd showered the travel grime off at Sydney airport and Evie was feeling more awake than she had been. Her body hadn't liked the extended flying hours, no matter how comfortable the seats had been. Her body didn't quite know which way was up, but her brain recognised Melbourne airport, the name of the hospital and Max, and that would have to do for now.

Max stood waiting for them, tension radiating from him in waves. Tension no longer radiated from Logan. Logan had left edgy behind a good sixteen hours ago in favour of an almost inhuman stillness and composure. Walling up his emotions, brick by brick, and the cabin crew had left him alone and so had Evie. The seats had been so far apart. There'd been no touching him.

He'd told her to get some sleep.

She'd tried.

'What's the latest?' asked Logan, for Max had been

texting them through updates every few hours, regardless of whether Logan could access them from the air.

'The swelling has stabilised,' Max offered gruffly. 'She's unconscious, but she has some partial awareness. She reacts to pain. She's come around a couple of times and called out a name but that's about it. The doctors say that's encouraging.'

'Whose name?' asked Logan.

'Yours.'

Logan turned away and Evie thought he might bolt back the way they'd come; through all the double doors and out of the hospital completely. But he stopped after a couple of steps as if held by some invisible force. His chest heaved and his hand came up to scrub at his face, forefinger and thumb, to press at his eyes and drag any moisture that might have gathered there away.

'You can go in,' said Max. 'There's chairs. You can sit.'

'Will you come in with me?' Logan's voice was so low she could barely hear him. He hadn't turned around. Evie didn't even know who he was talking to. She shared a glance with Max. He didn't know either.

Max gave the tiniest of shrugs, before replying. 'We can all go in. Whatever you want.'

Evie hugged her arms to her waist and stayed silent as Logan reluctantly turned back around, his bleak gaze seeking her out.

'Whatever you want,' she echoed quietly.

He nodded, just the slightest shift of his head. 'All of us.'

'Okay.'

There were six beds in the intensive care unit; six patients and ten times as many machines. Caroline Carmichael lay in the third bed on the left. There were tubes in her nose, tubes in her hand and wires running beneath the cover sheet. Max hadn't told them how swollen her face was or the way the colour was all kinds of wrong, black, crimson and blue—he could have warned them.

Evie hung back as Logan moved to the side of the bed and looked down at his mother.

'Speak to her,' suggested Max gruffly.

'Hey, Mum.' Logan didn't seem to have any idea what to say next. He shoved his hands in his jacket pockets, took them out a moment later and ran one hand around the back of his neck. 'Max said you wanted to see me.'

Caroline Carmichael's eyes twitched as if she was trying to open them, but Evie didn't think there was much chance of that. Not with the amount of swelling and bruising. God, the bruising. But then the older woman's mouth moved, as if she was trying to find her words.

'Logan?'

Caroline's hand twitched—the one with the tubes in it, and Logan reached for it, sliding his fingers underneath hers and curling them gently around hers.

'I'm here. I hear you got hit.' Logan's voice was nothing more than a tortured rumble. 'You should have got out of the way.'

'Couldn't,' said Caroline threadily. 'He went for her, see? Then her boy stepped up in front of her. Couldn't be that…coward.'

'You should have got out of the way,' repeated Logan doggedly.

'I stood up to him.'

'I know.' Logan's voice was barely audible this time

as he sank down into the chair beside the bed. 'You shouldn't have had to.'

'Thirty years too late,' whispered Caroline. 'About time...' Her mouth moved but her words didn't come to her immediately. 'Don't you think?'

Logan bowed his head and set his mother's hand to his cheek. His shoulders heaved and fat tears began to flow.

'Logan?' she whispered.

'I'm here.'

'I'm sorry.'

Caroline Carmichael had finally got her wish.

Evie watched in helpless silence, and so did Max, as Logan Black finally broke.

Three hours later and Evie sat in the intensive care waiting room, staring at the clock on the wall and the scratches in the floor and occasionally glancing over at Max who sat, eyes closed, with his legs stretched out before him and his hands in the pockets of his jeans. He had his head tilted back against the wall and every now and again he'd jerk as if he'd finally drifted into sleep only to remember where he was. Logan was still in the ward, sitting beside his mother; nothing else he could do as Caroline had slipped back into unconsciousness.

He'd leaned into the hand Evie had pressed between his shoulder blades when she told him she was going back out to the waiting room but he'd had no words for her. Just a nod.

Max didn't seem to have any words for her either.

'Did you know that he hit Logan too?' she asked finally, for it was playing on her mind.

Max opened his eyes to look at her. 'No.'

Lots of baggage, Logan. She'd said that to him once, long before she'd even known the half of it. She tried to think of the healing that might come of all of this. Caroline in there, desperate for absolution, and Logan giving it. Caroline finding her strength thirty years too late and paying for it in blood and bruises and believing it was worth it.

Hard to know what Logan believed, or what he felt beyond despair.

Max was still watching her, waiting to see what she would say next.

'You should go home,' she said. 'Get some rest. I can call you if there's any change.'

But Max just shook his head. 'I can sleep here.'

'You call that sleep?'

A tiny shrug and an even tinier half-smile. 'Polyphasic sleep experiment,' he murmured.

'I'm thinking eight solid hours would help more,' she replied dryly. 'Kit know where you are?'

Max nodded and closed his eyes again. Not going there. Butt out, Evie.

'What about food?' she asked next. 'When did you last have something decent to eat?'

'Define decent,' said Max without even opening his eyes.

'All right. I can't sit here. I'm going mad. I'm off on a food and coffee run. Works burger for you, if I can find one. Apple pie.'

'Hot chips with chicken salt,' murmured Max.

'Exactly. Comfort food. The really good bad-for-you stuff.'

Evie looked to those daunting double doors that led back through to the intensive care unit, wondering what

Logan might want by way of food or anything else. 'You think he's okay in there?'

'I think he's anything but okay, Evie,' offered Max gruffly. 'I just don't think there's anything anyone can do about it.'

Which was pretty much Evie's assessment of the situation too. 'Yeah, well. Maybe he's hungry.' Squaring her shoulders, Evie got up, took a deep breath and headed for Caroline Carmichael's bedside.

Logan had given up on sitting. He stood there, hands in his pockets and his gaze fixed on the monitors of the machines attached to his mother. He looked up as she came in and Evie's confidence grew at the flash of relief in his eyes and the tiniest tilt of his head.

'How is she?' she asked.

'No change.'

'I'm going on a food run. You want anything?'

'I'll come too.'

'You don't have to. That wasn't why I came in. Max's out in the waiting room trying desperately to stay awake. You're in here. I just want to stretch my legs as much as anything.' See whether it was daylight or dark outside. Her body couldn't remember.

'I'll come too,' Logan repeated, and followed her out into the waiting room and looked at his brother and frowned.

'Everything okay?' asked Max.

'You look beat.'

'Yeah, I—' Max ran his hands over his face. 'Yeah.'

'We're going to get some food. Bring it back here. Then you're going back to the house to get some sleep,' said Logan, every inch the big brother. 'Eight hours.

Don't show your face here again before then unless I call you.'

Max smiled faintly. 'Bossy.'

'Not exactly breaking news,' countered Logan.

So Evie went with Logan to a nearby café and they brought burgers and chips and coffee back to the waiting room—decaf for Max—and then Max left and Evie settled down to another long stint of sitting in the waiting room, this time with Logan, who took the seat next to hers.

He took her hand after a while. He played with her fingers and looked at the clock on the wall and the scratches on the floor and seemed content with silence, and Evie wanted to talk to him so desperately about so many things. She wanted to ask him if this was why he'd left her all those years ago. Whether it was the hospital that had freaked him out so, and the similarities between Evie's trip to Casualty and the trips he might have made to hospital waiting rooms as a child. She wanted to make this about *her*, and *their* relationship, and she wanted to ask him just how often he'd had to clean his mother up, or himself up, in the war zone that had been his home. But satisfying her curiosity seemed like such a selfish thing to do when Caroline Carmichael was in there fighting for her life and so Evie just sat there beside Logan and offered her hand in his or her thigh nudging his, her shoulder against his, because if anything could comfort Logan it was touch. Silence beamed their constant companion and when they did sometimes talk they said nothing of any consequence at all.

Two days later Caroline Carmichael regained consciousness and Max and Logan set about rearranging their lives around their mother's recovery. Evie watched them prepare to upend their lives for her, bring her home and keep her company here, take her to London or Sydney; whichever way they argued it, no way was Caroline Carmichael going to be alone.

They were staying at Caroline's house—making use of her cars and her facilities and eating her food. Logan and Max thought nothing of it. Evie thought it was a little bit presumptuous—not of Caroline's sons but of her—but Logan had flat out refused to let her stay in a hotel and Max had backed him and that was that.

She'd tried to make herself useful. She washed clothes and kept the fridge stocked, put new flowers in the vases and cleaned up around the home. Nothing big. Changing very little. Not her home.

She'd been on a supermarket run this evening—the fridge had been largely bare and she'd wanted to fill it before heading back to Sydney tomorrow. Max and Logan had been at the hospital when she'd headed out, but they were home when she returned, Max looking relieved and Logan wearing a scowl.

'Hey,' said Max with a smile that looked hard forced. 'We were just wondering where you were.'

Evie held up the grocery bags in hand. 'Most of the dinner ingredients are still in the car,' she offered by way of a hint. 'I thought we might have a nice meal to celebrate Caroline's most excellent prognosis, and, seeing as I'm leaving tomorrow, tonight's the night. Though it doesn't have to be if you've got something else on,' added Evie, because Logan was still scowling.

'I'll get the rest,' murmured Max and beat a hasty path for the door.

'Your phone wasn't on,' said Logan. 'You didn't say

where you were going. You don't know this neighbour-hood and it's seven o clock at night. Next time you *wait* for me and I'll come with you.'

Evie eyed him warily. 'Logan, I went grocery shopping. It happens a lot. It's *not* a two-person job. And I thought I'd be back before you. Next time I'll leave you a note.'

'And the phone?'

'The battery's probably run down. I'll charge it.'

But Logan still didn't look appeased.

'Look, Logan, there's concern for my well-being—which I appreciate—and then there's trying to control my every move—which is going to drive us both mad. Are we going to have a problem with this?'

Logan stared at her for what seemed like an eon, and then he let out a breath and ran a hand through his hair and turned away as Max came back in hauling grocery bags.

'All good?' asked Max, and Evie glared at him and Logan shot him a look that should have had a kill-warning attached. 'Great,' said Max. 'That's great.'

'Any more to come in?' asked Logan and Max nodded.

'Couple of bags.' And this time Logan disappeared to get them while Max started unpacking the ones he'd brought in. 'Hey…Evie…'

Evie waited for Max to spit out whatever he clearly didn't want to say.

'Look, I know Logan's being a little overprotective of you at the moment, and I know it chafes, but he's still pretty cut up about Mum. Can't you cut him some slack? Just for a little while.'

But Evie couldn't. 'I know what he's doing, Max.

I know why he's doing it. But I can't let Logan start down that road with me. It doesn't lead anywhere good.'

Max nodded unhappily. 'Your call. Just—go easy, okay?'

Evie nodded. 'I will. I'll try. This setting of boundaries within a relationship—it's new for me too.'

And then Logan came in with the rest of the groceries and Evie started to prepare dinner and both men stayed to help. The opening of wine became Max's job, Logan top and tailed crunchy green beans. Max put the stereo on in the other room and music wafted through to them, warm and mellow. They could use a bit of mellow, Logan most of all.

Because he simmered, there was no other word for it. And Evie spent a fair amount of time wondering just how much longer he was going to be able to keep a cap on the emotions threatening to consume him. The man needed a release valve. And he didn't seem to have one.

Talk turned to work. Carlo had been holding MEP together but he was needed out on a job. Logan had been doing what work he could from his mother's house but essentially he was relying on the management people he'd put in place to do their jobs and manage his business.

The doctors were saying that Caroline could come home from hospital in a couple of days. There'd been talk of neurologists, physical therapists, recreational therapists and psychiatrists and Caroline's sons had said yes to them all. Max and Logan were both sticking around to help get their mother settled.

'Maybe I need to think about moving operations back to Australia,' Logan said as he skewered thick steaks onto the frying plate, his attention only half on his words. Max stared and Evie stared and Logan looked at them both and said, 'What?'

'Nothing,' said Max and Evie in unison, but Evie stopped by the cooker and pulled Logan towards her for a kiss that spoke of wordless approval and a whole lot more.

'I know an exceptionally talented up-and-coming architect, should you be wanting to build yourself a better penthouse than that monstrosity in London,' offered Max once Evie had let Logan go.

'I thought you liked the monstrosity in London,' said Logan.

'I do,' said Max. 'But I can design and build better.'

'If we started from scratch I'd want a lot of specialist electrical work done,' said Logan with a stirrer's glance in his brother's direction. 'I'd need someone competent to oversee that part of the build.'

'We have one of those,' murmured Evie dulcetly. 'He's very amenable. I'm sure someone could persuade him to bid for the job.'

'If either of you think this conversation is going to get you any information whatsoever regarding the status of my relationship with a certain electrical subcontractor, you're wrong,' said Max.

'Relationship,' said Evie. 'You used the R word.'

'I did not.'

Oh, but he *had*. And he was blushing because he knew it.

'Anyway,' muttered Max. 'Kit's got a big government contract lined up in PNG. He's not going to be around much.' Max looked to Evie. 'He wants to know if we want in on the build.'

'In PNG?' First Evie had heard of it. 'What sort of build?'

'It's a—'

'No.' Logan's voice cut across Max's, heavy with warning. 'You don't want to be building anything in PNG. As for Evie, she *certainly* doesn't want to be working there. It's not safe.'

'Well,' said Max, and shot Logan a troubled glance. 'That's one opinion.'

'It's not opinion. It's fact.'

'*You* work there,' countered Max mildly.

'I consult there every so often as a favour to a friend. I don't send my people there and I certainly don't plan to do business there. There are easier ways to lose the skin off my back.'

'What sort of build?' Evie asked again, and Logan turned on her.

'Did you hear me?' he asked icily.

'Yes.' Evie kept her voice smooth and even. 'Did you hear me? Because much as I appreciate your input on this, Logan, I'm interested in the details. Once I hear them, I may even agree with you. I may not. I may wonder what Kit is doing mixed up in this if it's as dangerous as you say. What I'm *not* going to do is let you speak for me.'

Logan said nothing.

'Logan,' she said softly. 'You have a point. The delivery's a little off, but I do hear you. Your opinion matters to me. I'm interested in hearing it. But then I get to make up my own mind.' Evie smiled a little, hoping to coax forth a smile in return but Logan was having none of it. 'You worry that I might be too meek for you.

I keep telling you that I will hold my own against you if need be. Well, this is me. Holding my own.'

But Logan was done talking. He picked up the car keys that she'd dropped on the bench, his jaw set and his every movement oh-so-carefully controlled. 'I'm going to get some beer. We're out.'

No, they weren't. And Evie was done with this man bottling everything up inside. 'So that's your answer to disagreement, is it?' Evie didn't want to do this. Not in front of Max. Not at all. But she'd had enough of tippy-toeing around the real issue. She'd had enough of Logan living in fear. 'When are you going to stop running away from your emotions, Logan? When are you going to realise that people argue, lovers argue, and emotions can run hot, *should* run hot, at times, and that it's not the end of the world?'

Logan stopped, turned towards her and she met him glare for glare.

'Stay,' she coaxed softly. 'Argue your point. Engage with me in debate.'

'I've said all I have to say, Evie. I've made my position very clear.'

'You argued your point for all of thirty seconds. What's the matter, Logan? Scared that if you stay you'll lose your temper?'

'No.' Logan shook his head, never mind the burning heat already in his eyes.

'I think that's exactly what you're scared of. What *does* happen when you lose your temper, Logan? What happens when you finally let go?'

'I don't.' Eyes like bruises and still he stared her down.

'Scared you're going to do what your daddy did and

use your fists to force obedience? Put me in hospital? Is that what you're scared of? Is that why you run?'

'Evie—' protested Max.

'No,' said Logan tightly. 'Evie, no.'

But he'd taken her to hospital once and Evie now knew exactly why he'd run. Tortured, this man of hers. He was still running. 'All that anger. All that pain. Wrap it up in a fist and call it an accident, but it never is—is it, Logan? It can't possibly be an accident if you're involved. It's in your blood.'

'No.'

'Yes. You know exactly how it's done. And it's your turn now. You won't be able to stop yourself.'

'I will.'

And Evie steeled her nerves and stepped up into his space, in his face, and pushed him some more. 'You sure about that?'

'I am *not* my father's son, do you hear me?' roared Logan. 'No matter what you do, no matter how much you disagree with me, I will never, *ever* raise my hand to you in anger.'

'I know.' Evie reached for him, one hand to the base of his neck and the other hand to his back, hugging him hard and waiting, waiting for what seemed like for ever before his arms came around her and tightened. 'I know,' she whispered against his neck. 'I've always known. I just wasn't sure *you* knew.'

She felt the tremors in him as his arms tightened around her. 'Well, I sure as hell know *now*.'

'That was kind of the point.'

'Hell, Evie.' Even Max sounded thoroughly shaken. 'Couldn't you have just asked?'

'Been there, done that.' Evie held Logan tighter and felt the beat of his heart against the thundering of her own. 'Didn't work.'

Logan rescued the steaks, Max put the food on the plates and they took them through to the dining room. The music still played soft and mellow, but the mellow mood was gone and Evie didn't think it was about to reappear any time soon.

She needed the reassurance of Logan's touch but there was food to be eaten and jobs to discuss, so Evie contented herself with tangling her legs around Logan's beneath the table and taking from that what comfort she could.

'So…' said Logan, with a half-smile for Evie and a level glance for his brother. 'How serious are you about this job in PNG?'

'I'm serious about Kit,' said Max with a wary glance in Logan's direction. 'Don't particularly think we need the job. It's a government offices refurb job. Sounds simple. Profitable. But I'm absolutely aware that it could be a mess and that the last thing we want to do is tie up our resources.'

'I can make some enquiries,' offered Logan. 'Put you in touch with some people who do business there. They can run through some of the challenges with you. It'll help.'

'Evie?' said Max. 'What do you say?'

'Truthfully, I don't see much in it for us. It's maintenance work. There's no status in it, just the headaches that come with having to fix other people's mistakes and a distant and sometimes dangerous work location. We're not that desperate for money.'

'We owe Logan ten million dollars, Evie.'

'No, Logan's ten million dollars is sitting in MEP's bank account and he'll get it back the minute the civic centre build is out of the ground. There's a difference. Besides, in two years' time when your trust fund turns over you won't be worried about money at all.' Evie eyed Max steadily, looking for a reaction and finding it in the tiny frown that framed her business partner's eyes. 'You asked for my opinion and I'm giving it. This PNG job sounds like stress we don't need. However... I do understand that it's not always about money or prestige. There's the working with Kit factor. Covering his back so that he stays safe and gets in and out with minimum fuss. That's a factor I don't know how to weigh up.'

'Some people might say that's not a factor I should be bringing to the business table,' said Max.

'Not me.'

'You sure?'

'Max, you've been working around my emotional baggage, and Logan's, for months. It's affected my work. MEP's finances. Your relationship with your family. I think I can cut you some slack.' Evie rolled her eyes. Even Logan looked amused, and wasn't that a welcome sight? 'It's entirely possible that part of the appeal of working in PNG is that you'd be getting *away* from me,' she continued

'What? And miss all this?' Max smiled, wide and warm and this time so did Logan.

'Get Kit to call me,' said Logan. 'I can help.'

Max nodded and more food got eaten. Not exactly smooth sailing here tonight and it probably never would be—not with Logan in the mix—but they were making progress. Logan had put his demons on leash and brought them to heel for her. Hard not to get a little breathless about that. 'We good?' she asked him quietly.

'Yeah.' Logan's gaze slid to her mouth and need flared fierce and bright inside her.

They'd argued and made up. Surely there was still room for crazy hot make-up sex in there somewhere. Because she wanted her hands on him, skin on skin, she needed his touch and—

'Stop it,' said Max firmly, and waved a bread and butter plate in front of Evie's face. 'Evie, stop looking at him like that. Don't encourage him. Logan doesn't *need* any encouragement in that direction.'

'Not that it hurts,' said Logan and the rough need in his voice made Evie altogether twitchy deep down inside.

'Don't look at her.' Max turned to his brother. 'Eyes on the plate. This is a family meal we're having here and I for one want to keep my appetite.'

'Food. Yes.' Right. Evie took the plate, wrenched herself out of devouring-Logan-land and schooled her features to reflect what she hoped was baffled innocence. 'Really, Max. It was only a little look. Slightly appreciative.'

'Highly inflammatory,' corrected Max. 'Let's have a toast.'

'To fires?'

'To family,' said Max. 'And it isn't just about blood.' They drank to that and Max gave them another one. 'To my mother's speedy recovery and good health.' They drank to that, too. 'And to my brother.'

'What for?' asked Logan gruffly.

'For being you,' said Max, and they drank to that,

too, sat in the small dining room at a table meant for four and Max started talking about speedboats on Sydney harbour and Logan relaxed and his smiles came warm and easy. How many people saw this side of Logan? The unguarded heart and the tumble of generosity.

Not many.

Safe, thought Evie, grasping at the edges of her understanding of this man. Logan felt safe here with his brother and with her.

They made it an early night. Half ten when they headed for bed, Evie having made herself at home in Logan's bedroom days ago, hanging clothes in his cloakroom and putting her toothbrush next to his.

He hadn't complained.

It had become almost a ritual, this act of showering and putting night clothes on just so Logan could peel them off.

He was sitting on the edge of the bed, elbows on his knees and his hands crossed loosely in front of him, when Evie emerged from the bathroom. He watched in silence as she headed his way.

'I'm sorry about today,' he offered when she was close enough to touch him and touch him she did, running her hand through the silky softness of his hair and tilting his head back, ever so gently. 'I lost my way.'

'No harm done,' she murmured and slid her hand to his face next and dragged the pad of her thumb across his full lower lip. 'A power of good done and you need to know that I won't ever do that to you again. I had a point to make and I've made it. I know what you are, Logan. I know what you're not. I can handle you, everything about you. And you can handle me.'

'Blind crazy about you, Evie,' he said raggedly.

'Right back at you.'

Logan reached for her, wrapping his arms around her waist and dragging her between his legs. Evie closed her eyes and let out a gasp as he turned his head slightly and pressed his lips into the base of her palm and then his tongue streaked out and skittered against her wrist.

The man was an expert at making her lose her way.

Evie tipped forward, knowing that if Logan hadn't wanted to go down on his back he wouldn't have. He wouldn't have let her look her fill if he hadn't liked her eyes on him. And then she wound her fingers through his and pinned his hands above his head and pressed whisper-light kisses from the corner of his eye to the edge of his lips before tasting him with her tongue.

She wanted to take her time. Render him aching and pliant and *hers*. Teasing kisses made way for longer play. Drugging kisses that left his lips shiny and swollen and she moved on to his neck and felt a swift surge of satisfaction when he tilted his head to allow her better access.

If this man had a weakness it was touch. He shuddered beneath it, and every now and then—in mildest measure—she served it up with a nip of pain, and, oh, he liked that. He came undone on that.

'I've got you,' she whispered more than once, and watched his lips part and hot colour stain his cheeks. 'Watching out for you.' With every whispered word and knowing touch, Evie unravelled him just that little bit more.

'I love you,' she whispered against his lips as she straddled him and took him deep inside and he closed his eyes and let her lead the way.

CHAPTER ELEVEN

'STAY,' murmured LOGAN the following morning as Evie packed her travel bag in readiness for her flight to Sydney. The bag sat on the end of Logan's bed. Logan was still in the bed, sleep-softened and way too appealing for his own good. He'd surrendered so completely to her last night and Evie had taken the sweetest satisfaction in getting him completely and utterly lost to everything but sensation before bringing him home. She knew this game, knew how to wield the power he'd given her. She'd been taught by a master.

This morning, however, the balance of who led and who followed was shifting between them again.

'I can't stay,' she answered lightly. 'Max is staying and someone needs to get back to run MEP and that someone is me.'

Evie didn't want to argue about this. She wasn't about to change her mind. They'd already argued about Evie taking a taxi to the airport and Evie had won. There was no need for Logan to drive her to the airport. The man could use the sleep.

'Stay anyway.' There was no mistaking the rawness in his voice and it made Evie pause in her packing. Some of that rawness could be attributed to the intensity of last night's lovemaking, but not all. Maybe he was scared of being left alone.

But he wouldn't be alone.

'You're going to be busy too.' Evie abandoned the messy tossing of clothes into her case in favour of crawling across the bed and kneeling at Logan's side. She stroked the pale skin of his inner forearm with her fingertips and felt him relax ever so slightly. She brought his hand up, pressed her lips to his knuckles and felt him relax just that little bit more. 'Bringing your mother home. Getting her settled. She's not going to want a stranger in her home and you've got all sorts of family stuff to decide. I'm not a part of that process. That one's all yours and you'll be fine. You'll all be fine. The decisions you make will be good ones. You'll see.'

Logan clasped her hand in his and sat up, nudging her shoulder with his when he drew level with her. 'The decisions this family makes about the future are going to affect you too, Evie. You and me. Your work and Max's. You *could* stay. Be a part of the decision making.'

But Evie didn't want to be. 'I'm not very good at family stuff, Logan. I barely make contact with my own.'

'Any particular reason why?'

'No. My family's just…scattered. There's bits of it everywhere and I'm not anyone's priority. It's easier if I stay away.'

'You're *my* priority,' he said with another bump for her shoulder, drawing her gaze and keeping it. 'If I come back to Australia I want to base my work in Sydney. Live in Sydney. Because of you. You said you wanted more from me, but I don't know how to measure it. I just know that if you let me I'll take everything you have

to give. I'm greedy like that. So I'm asking you now—
before I put plans in motion that affect other people—
whether you want me living in Sydney and demanding
more of your time and everything else.'

'Yes.' Gut response, well in advance of rational
thought. 'Yes, I'd like that. Didn't you get a ranty phone
call from me demanding more of you?'

'Yes, but that was before you *had* me, 24/7. Maybe
you've changed your mind.'

'I haven't changed my mind.'

'You sure?'

'Positive.'

Logan's expression moved from searchingly intent to
boyishly pleased in an instant. He threw back the sheet,
scrambled out of bed and headed stark naked for the en
suite. Nothing boyish about the play of muscles in his
back, though, or the tight globes of his buttocks. Evie
tilted her head the better to appreciate the view. 'Why
aren't you going back to sleep?' she called after him.

'Why would I be doing that?' The sound of the
shower running followed soon after. 'When I'm taking you to the airport.'

Life and Logan treated Evie exceptionally well over the
next few weeks. Logan's mother came home and pressed
charges and began to mend. More weeks passed, weeks
that turned into months as Logan relocated his business
to Sydney, kept his Perth office running, and treated
flying to Melbourne to see his mother as if it were no
more onerous than stepping on a bus. Different mindset
from Evie's. When money was no object a lot of things
could happen with speed and relative ease.

A short-term lease on a fully furnished inner-city

penthouse apartment for Logan. A lease on the apartment across the hall for his mother and Caroline began to travel to Sydney for a couple of days each week instead of her boys travelling to Melbourne to be with her.

It had been years since a female figure had played any more than a token role in Evie's life, but Caroline Carmichael seemed determined to fix that, inviting Evie to lunches and brunches and shopping—oh, the *clothes* Logan's mother could afford. Elegant and flattering. Evie had discovered a brand-new obsession. Two pieces she bought for herself, with Caroline giving them the Carmichael seal of approval, and after that she had to stop, because that was her treat for the year and she couldn't afford more. She wouldn't let Caroline buy more for her either, no matter how often the older woman offered to.

'Shopping with your mother feeds my fascination for how some women can pull separate pieces of clothing together to create a look that makes mere mortals sigh with envy,' said Evie one evening when they were at Caroline's apartment and Logan had asked Evie how the late-night shopping trip had gone.

'Enrique's got sales on as of next Wednesday,' Caroline murmured dulcetly. 'He told me in strictest confidence. Half price. We should at least go and have a look for a coat for you. You're going to need one out on site.'

'She has a coat for when she's on site,' argued Max, for he was at his mother's place too.

'He's right,' said Evie. 'It's dark blue and puffy, with fluorescent yellow stripes. Goes with the hard hat.' Evie grinned as Caroline shuddered. 'I'll model it for you tomorrow when you come to visit the civic centre site. I might even be able to rustle up a hard hat for you too.'

'Why are you visiting the civic centre site?' Max asked his mother. 'We've barely started the foundation work. It's just a hole in the ground.'

'Architects,' teased Evie. 'They're all about the frills. Absolutely no regard for the achievements along the way. Trust me, Caroline. This is a beautiful hole in the ground.'

'And you're going to admire it why?' Logan asked his mother.

'I want to see what Evangeline does,' said his mother. 'Besides keep you two in check.'

'That is a full-time job in and of itself,' said Evie with a hard-put-upon sigh. 'Did you hear that Logan's now looking for a house with harbour frontage? And Max is encouraging him? And they're talking about buying a boat.'

'A really good boat,' said Max. 'To go with the excellently located house.'

'Logan, you didn't tell me this,' said his mother.

'But I would have,' he countered smoothly. 'I was just waiting for the half-price coat sale to end.'

'Excuses, excuses,' said Evie. 'Logan, you need a high-maintenance harbourside mansion all to yourself about as much as I need a five-thousand-dollar coat.'

'Well, maybe I just want one.' Logan smiled, slow and sure. 'You want me to buy you a coat while I'm at it? Half price.'

Sneaky man. 'No. No one's buying me a coat. I have a coat and it works just fine.'

'What about jewellery?' asked Caroline. 'Can someone buy you that? Brand-new? No memories attached? Because I have. Bought you something, I mean.'

'Really?' Evie eyed Caroline warily. The last time

Caroline had tried to give Evie jewellery things hadn't gone well for them.

'Now you're scaring her,' said Max.

'There's nothing to be scared of,' said Caroline. 'No ulterior motive whatsoever, beyond a thank you for looking after my house and my garden while I was unwell. It's just a little gift.'

Evie looked to Logan and he quirked his eyebrow as if to say why not?

'Come,' coaxed Caroline and handed a bunch of table napkins to Max. 'It's in my room. We'll do it now. It'll only take a moment.'

'Little tip for you, Evie,' murmured Max, thoroughly amused. 'We're twenty-two storeys up. If you don't like it and toss it out the window, it's gone.'

'I'm not *that* uncivilised.'

And then she caught Logan's darkly amused gaze once more and his look said, yes, yes, she was. And he liked her that way.

'I can behave,' she murmured on her way past Logan, and he caught her hand and pulled her close and pressed a kiss to her temple.

'Do I need to buy you jewellery too?' he asked softly.

'No. I just want your beating heart and your crooked soul.' Evie slipped away with a smile and Logan let her go. Easy to let go these days when she knew that come nightfall Logan would be sharing her bed and come morning he'd be in the kitchen begging the coffee machine for coffee, thick and black. Life these past few weeks had been rich and full and fun and Evie aimed to keep it that way.

'In here, Evie,' Caroline said from her bedroom as Evie stepped into the hallway and followed the sound of the older woman's voice. Evie hovered in the bed-room doorway. The apartment was far more imper-sonal than Caroline's Toorak residence, but the bedroom was still the other woman's personal sleeping space and Evie didn't want to intrude, no matter how relaxed she'd grown in the older woman's company these past few weeks.

'Caroline, you didn't have to do this.'

'I know,' said Caroline and her eyes were bright. 'But I wanted to.'

'I did very little when it came to looking after your house.'

'I wanted to,' Caroline repeated firmly and held out a blue box with a white satin ribbon. 'And it's not about the house, Evie. You know that. Please. Open it.'

Evie tugged gently on the ribbon, taking her time—still wary, just a little bit, of Caroline's motives.

'First time I ever met you, you and Max had a con-versation about a non-existent engagement ring that made me smile. Diamond, you said when he asked you what it was you wanted. White. I liked your quick think-ing and I did like your style. Don't worry,' urged Caro-line as the ribbon fell away and Evie eyed her warily. 'It's not an engagement ring. That's not for me to sort out. This is simply about the making of new memories between us when it comes to the giving of jewellery. New memories to replace those I'd rather not remember. I learned this trick a long time ago and it has always stood me in good stead. So...' Caroline straightened her shoulders and lifted her chin, but her eyes remained full of entreaty. 'Let's make a new memory, Evie. You and me.'

'All right,' said Evie. 'I'm in.'

Evie lifted the lid of the box and stared down at the bangle nestled within. Oh, boy. Platinum, Evie suspected. Platinum strands of varying thicknesses criss-crossing over and sidling up against one another all a tangle. In amongst the spaces between the strands sat a scattering of diamonds of all different sizes, some of them at least a carat, some of them only a quarter of that size. Brilliant cut, the lot of them, and there *were* a lot of them. Every last one of them a pure and blazing white. 'Oh, boy. I am *so* in.'

'Do you like it?'

'Oh, yes.' And Evie thought Caroline had excellent taste in clothes. 'I love it. But it's so delicate. And... amazing.' Expensive, was what she wanted to say. 'Where on earth will I wear it?'

'Anywhere,' coaxed Caroline. 'Wear it with what you have on now. Enjoy it. Take pleasure in it.'

Evie was wearing jeans and a vivid pink, fitted short-sleeved shirt and she stifled a giggle as she fished the bangle from its box and slipped it on and sighed with delight.

'Yes,' said Caroline. 'Just like that. And I will be content.'

'So show us,' said Max when Evie and Caroline reappeared in the living room.

Evie showed them and Logan said, 'Like it?' and Max rolled his eyes.

'It's beautiful,' said Evie.

'It's a cunning plot to get you used to luxury living and harbourside mansions,' said Max, and Caroline smiled and Evie figured that there was a slim possibility Max was right. Not that she wanted to acknowledge it.

'Hey, you're the one who wants a really big boat.'

'Doesn't need to be big,' said Max. 'I didn't say big. It just has to be good.'

'Fast,' added Logan.

'Fast definitely falls within the definition of good,' said Max.

'Corruption is rife around here,' said Evie.

And so was the love.

Two months later, Logan still hadn't found himself the perfect home. He looked at whatever homes Max flagged for him and he usually dragged Evie along to look at them too. Invariably, the properties boasted waterfront access and harbour bridge views, piers and boat moorings. You know…for the yacht.

Easy to forget—when Logan was sprawled out on Evie's sofa in her little apartment—just how wealthy he truly was.

Not so easy when he went home hunting.

'Why do you even need a home this big? There's only one of you,' Evie grumbled as she stomped through yet another harbourside wonder. He had a key to her apartment and a clothes rack full of his clothes in her bedroom. If he wasn't travelling, ten-to-one Logan could be found at her place. 'Why not just move in with me and save yourself the trouble?'

'Home office,' he murmured. 'I want one. This place has two. And a library.'

'Greedy.'

'Evie, I'm working from a pile of paperwork stacked on your desk. That's when I haven't left half of it at my place. We need more room. *I* need more room.'

'Is this an ownership thing?'

'Absolutely. And a size thing. Possibly a status thing. Definitely a let's buy somewhere together thing.'

'What?' He'd snuck that one in fast. But there was no way she was going to let it pass without comment. 'But…I have a red ceiling. You like my red ceiling. And, more realistically, there is no way I could ever afford to buy a house like this with you.'

'Proportional investment,' murmured Logan, his eyes lighting up as if it were Christmas at the sight of the indoor lap pool and spa. Evie's eyes might have opened a little wider at the sight of them too. 'You live a comfortable life, Evie, and I'm not trying to dismiss it. I'm a huge fan of your fire pole. But here you could have a flying fox from the bedroom to the jetty.'

'Floating tennis court,' she suggested with a grin. 'I could make you make it happen.'

'You could. I'd never deny it,' he said, looking back over his shoulder at her with a con man's grin. 'C'mon, Evie. I like this one. Keep your apartment if it'll assuage your need for independence but please…' He knew exactly how much she liked to please him. 'Let's buy this one together.'

'You could buy it ten times over all by yourself.'

'Yes, and if I did you'd think of it as mine. I'm ready for something that's ours, Evie. Are you?'

'I don't know. I'm thinking about it,' she said, looking down through the branches of a gum tree to the extensive gardens below. 'Is there a doghouse?'

'Why? You thinking of relegating me to it already?'

'No.' Neither of them had been in the doghouse for quite some time. Oh, he could still do a mighty fine possessive wolf impersonation, and he did—most decidedly—have a superbly honed skill set when it came

to getting his own way. But he did his damndest to listen to her views and accommodate them, and besides…
Evie had a powerful negotiating weapon of her own.

Love.

Only three people in that small, select group for
whom Logan would do anything. Give anything. Cut
out his heart and lay it at their feet.

And one of them was Evie.

He'd turn his back on this place if Evie asked it of
him. He'd downsize his life so that Evie would feel more
comfortable in it. He wasn't asking her to be a trophy
wife who catered to his every need. He wasn't asking
her to cut back on her workload. Apart from a comment
about MEP needing another project manager—which
they did—Logan trusted her to sort out her work com-
mitments for herself. What he *was* asking for was a
commitment to sharing a future with him.

'Maybe I can get your brother to build us a doghouse
if there isn't one already,' she said thoughtfully. 'Maybe
he can convert the boathouse. Mates' rates. I'm pretty
sure Kit would do the wiring for free. Maybe that could
be my initial contribution towards buying this place.
That and the paint.'

'Why would we need paint?'

'Logan, every wall in this place is white. I'm planning on living with you in glorious love-soaked Tech-
nicolor. Did you notice that there's a nursery? And an
abundance of bedrooms?'

'I noticed,' he said gruffly.

'Want to help me fill them?'

Logan's smile came slow and full of promise.
'When?'

'Not straight away. But some day.'

'We do that and I'm going to want to put a ring on your finger, Evie.'

'Traditionalist.'

'It's an ownership thing.'

'Give you an inch and you'll take ten thousand miles.'

Damn but he had the sweetest smile. 'You can handle it.'

'Yes, I can.'

'You're very smug,' murmured Logan as he stalked towards her.

'It's a love thing. It happens when love is returned in full. With change. Speaking of which…did you want to put an offer in on this house today? Because I've got a dollar on me. No, wait. I've got two.' Evie patted her pockets, not protesting at all when Logan backed her up against the pool room door and claimed her wrists and pinned them above her head. She was going to like sharing pool space with Logan. She was going to like it a lot.

'Evie.'

Evie had no defences whatsoever against the way he whispered her name as if all the colours of his world were wrapped up in it. His lips began playing merry havoc with her pulse points and she had no defence against that either. 'What were we talking about again?' she asked breathlessly.

'This house.' Logan slid his lips across to nibble at her ear. 'Our children.' Another nibble. 'And you just agreed to marry me.'

'I did?'

'Devil's honour.'

They could argue about the devil's honour later. 'Let's go tell the estate agent we want the house,' she murmured. 'Two dollars ought to be enough to convince him of my sincerity, shouldn't it?'

Logan's soft laughter rippled along her skin as he freed her wrists and she wrapped her arms around his neck. 'It's going to take a little more than that.'

'That's okay,' she murmured and offered up her mouth for his kiss. 'I also have you.'

* * * * *

ROMANCE

MEDICAL

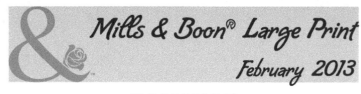

Mills & Boon® Large Print

February 2013

ROMANCE

HISTORICAL

MEDICAL

ROMANCE

Playing the Dutiful Wife	Carol Marinelli
The Fallen Greek Bride	Jane Porter
A Scandal, a Secret, a Baby	Sharon Kendrick
The Notorious Gabriel Diaz	Cathy Williams
A Reputation For Revenge	Jennie Lucas
Captive in the Spotlight	Annie West
Taming the Last Acosta	Susan Stephens
Island of Secrets	Robyn Donald
The Taming of a Wild Child	Kimberly Lang
First Time For Everything	Aimee Carson
Guardian to the Heiress	Margaret Way
Little Cowgirl on His Doorstep	Donna Alward
Mission: Soldier to Daddy	Soraya Lane
Winning Back His Wife	Melissa McClone
The Guy To Be Seen With	Fiona Harper
Why Resist a Rebel?	Leah Ashton
Sydney Harbour Hospital: Evie's Bombshell	Amy Andrews
The Prince Who Charmed Her	Fiona McArthur

MEDICAL

NYC Angels: Redeeming The Playboy	Carol Marinelli
NYC Angels: Heiress's Baby Scandal	Janice Lynn
St Piran's: The Wedding!	Alison Roberts
His Hidden American Beauty	Connie Cox

Mills & Boon® Large Print

March 2013

ROMANCE

A Night of No Return	Sarah Morgan
A Tempestuous Temptation	Cathy Williams
Back in the Headlines	Sharon Kendrick
A Taste of the Untamed	Susan Stephens
The Count's Christmas Baby	Rebecca Winters
His Larkville Cinderella	Melissa McClone
The Nanny Who Saved Christmas	Michelle Douglas
Snowed in at the Ranch	Cara Colter
Exquisite Revenge	Abby Green
Beneath the Veil of Paradise	Kate Hewitt
Surrendering All But Her Heart	Melanie Milburne

HISTORICAL

How to Sin Successfully	Bronwyn Scott
Hattie Wilkinson Meets Her Match	Michelle Styles
The Captain's Kidnapped Beauty	Mary Nichols
The Admiral's Penniless Bride	Carla Kelly
Return of the Border Warrior	Blythe Gifford

MEDICAL

Her Motherhood Wish	Anne Fraser
A Bond Between Strangers	Scarlet Wilson
Once a Playboy…	Kate Hardy
Challenging the Nurse's Rules	Janice Lynn
The Sheikh and the Surrogate Mum	Meredith Webber
Tamed by her Brooding Boss	Joanna Neil